THE LAST
GREAT
PUB CRAWL
A novel by
John Shane

'When the elephant walks, many creatures howl after him, but he does not turn back.'

Indian Proverb.

Printed by Print Logic Limited
Foley Estate, Hereford.

ISBN 0 905198 02 6

A novel by

JOHN SHANE

With illustrations by

DAVID BARRINGTON

This Book was produced with the help of a grant from West Midlands Arts

The Full Moon Press *Westhope— Herefordshire.*

PART ONE : THE VILLAGE

PART TWO : THE CITY

I (in an unofficial capacity be it noted.)

Walter Arthur Vowles,

595th. Mayor of Hereford

do hereby grant and award this

Poetic Licence

No. 76372023

to

John Shane

Permitting him to render description of the pubs, alehouses and hostelries of our historic city, and to further write humorously so long as it be without malicious intent about this city and its good people, for the purpose of his book entitled;

"The Last Great Pub Crawl."

And may I recommend this book most strongly to one and all. W. A. Vowles

Signed this 1st **day of** November **in the Year of Our Lord One thousand, nine hundred and seventy-s**

My thanks are due to all the friends whose support and encouragement have helped this book to be born:
Nancy Henderson of W.M.A., for her cheerful chuckle, the Carr family for the typewriter and the use of the kitchen table, the Ferris wheel for tea and sympathy, Barbara Smith for coffee and conversation, Simon S. for points of law, Robin for getting me up in the morning, Jolene for putting me on to the illustrator, Kay for her letters, Sarah for jam and Tai-Chi, Nicki for nonsense, Ma and Pa for being Ma and Pa, and, of course, the publicans of the various pubs for pulling the pumps.

Here's to you all, and to all the others too numerous to mention! !

J.S. November 1st 1976

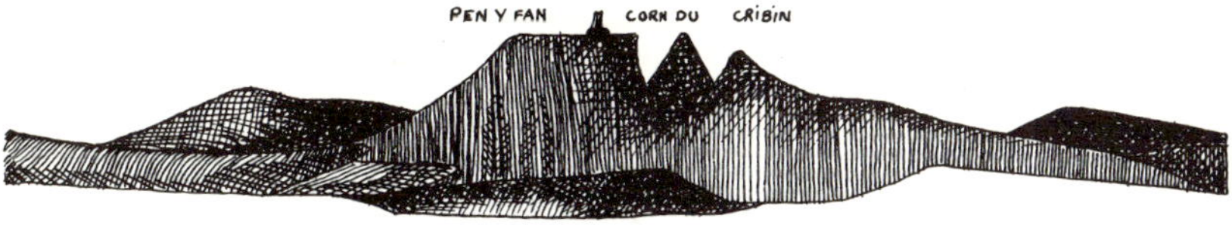
PEN Y FAN
CORN DU
CRIBIN

Part One

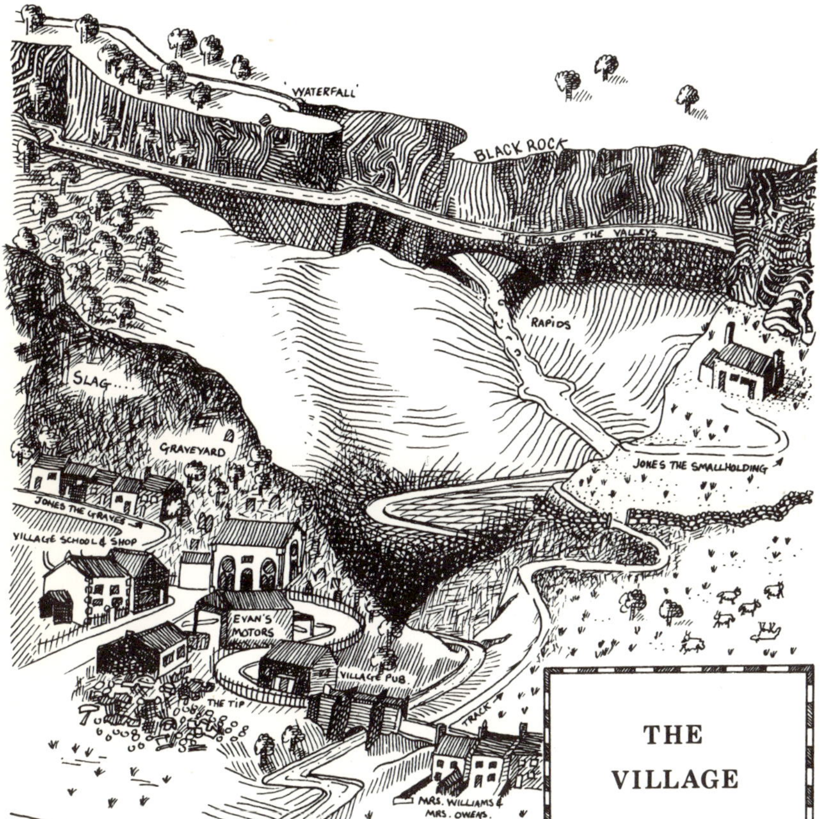
'WATERFALL'
BLACK ROCK
THE HEADS OF THE VALLEYS
RAPIDS
SLAG....
GRAVEYARD
JONES THE SMALLHOLDING
JONES THE GRAVES
VILLAGE SCHOOL & SHOP
EVAN'S MOTORS
VILLAGE PUB
THE TIP
TRACK
MRS. WILLIAMS & MRS. OWENS.
THE VILLAGE

The Three Old Friends

There is no reason why this story should be told; nor is there any reason why it should not be. It is like a flower that opens just for the love of turning itself inside out, unconcerned whether anyone watches.

No great heroes stalk these pages, to amaze us with their dazzling achievements. No Kings and Queens carouse by candlelight in enchanted castles. No victories are won by charismatic generals with rows of ribbons on their chests. No black misdeeds are plotted by fanged and exotic villains lurking in the shadows. No mountain peaks are scaled and conquered at great peril, and risk to life and limb. No frontiers of science are expanded by eccentric professors, ahead of their time, and badly misunderstood, obliged to struggle on in laboratories full of cobwebs and bats.

Such things are, of course, all the stuff of histories, and no doubt history would pass by the three old men whose story this is, shrugging them off as far too ordinary to contend with, and dismissing their village with a sniff.

If this summer will be remembered at all, it will be remembered, perhaps, as The Summer of the Drought. And like so many little villages in the Welsh hills, the village in this story, and its inhabitants, were more accustomed to the traditional British umbrella and macintosh summer, providing plenty of rainy days, and showers even on some of the warm ones.

The scorching heat, day after day, caught them unprepared. As the hammer of the sun beat down on the corrugated roof of the chapel, heating it up like a griddle till you could fry an egg, and perhaps some bacon on it, you would still find Mrs. Owen and Mrs. Williams hanging out woolly jumpers and woolly underwear on their back garden lines.

"You never do know, now, do you? " Mrs. Williams could be heard to remark, as the temperature continued to soar.

And it was the same everywhere in this small tightly knit community. Evans Motor's Garage still had anti-freeze prominently on display, and sold some. Minnie the Shop, almost invisible as usual behind her counter festooned with every imaginable item, still sold wellington boots amid the fuming cheese. And the souwesters, galoshes and raincapes still remained hanging from the hooks in the ceiling all summer. While the cats dozed, and snored, trying to keep cool among the newspapers, magazines and cigarettes somehow crammed into Minnie's tiny treasure store, she sold as much soup as she did ice lollies and pop, even on the hottest day of the year.

Not that the village didn't trust the weather you understand. It's just that you never do know, now, do you?

Jones the Graves, Sexton to the chapel these last forty-five years, sweltering in the graveyard, watched his lovely green grass turn brown, thought of the emptying reservoirs in the next valley, and decided not to water the Dead.

Walking home towards his little terraced cottage in Coronation Row, with its neat net curtains and tidy lace on the backs of the armchairs, he approached Evan's Garage at the crossroads in the centre of the village.

Evans Motors, also known as Evans the Garage, a round and roly-poly man, dapper and jovial, balding on top and greying at the sides, was stood by his brand new petrol pumps, proud as a king in the orderly forecourt of his kingdom.

Who would guess that behind this tidy front, behind those big doors with the name Evans proudly emblazoned on them, behing the smartly painted garage buildings, chaos lurked, ever threatening to take over.

Evans was a man balanced on a razor's edge, if a king, a king forever struggling to hold back the tide . . . the tide of disorder. The garage buildings hid his great guilty secret. Lurking behind them was a huge pile of rusting metal, mouldering machines, spare parts that might just come in handy sometime, and had stayed where they were for years, and years and years.

Bits of bikes, bedsprings, hulks of long forgotton engines, nested in by birds, overgrown by weeds, here was a vast elephant's graveyard full of relics of the dinosaurs of the first great machine age. Evans the Garage never could throw anything away, and this great mound continued growing like a pyramid, dwarfing the spruce modern bungalow that was his home.

Rumours spread in the village pub that Evans would have himself buried beneath this accumulated treasure, rather than commit himself to the care of Jones the Graves, his lifelong friend, whom he could now see coming up the cobbled street towards him.

Passing a rainwater butt, empty in the heat, Jones the Graves was riddled with imaginary machine gun fire by a small boy using it as a bunker to ambush just such elderly invaders in his comic book war. The Graves, a small, almost elfin man, with boots, cloth cap and ears all seeming too big for his bony, wiry frame, was always as smart as any general, always neat and tidy.And now, ducking good naturedly, he returned this gunfire with a grin. Then he carefully crossed the street, marked out with the white lines that he himself had so meticulously repainted every year, and finally, he greeted the friend of his schooldays.

"Hello, the Motors. How's Evans today? Still piling up scrap, I see. One day the whole lot'll come tumbling down on the village, I tell you, and kill us all in our beds. Remember Aberfan, and remember, I warned you."

This teasing banter was a permanent feature of the relationship, a village tradition, not lightly to be laid aside, and it was now Evan's turn to reply in kind.

"You're twenty-five seconds behind time coming away from work, Jones the Graves, boyo, that old gold watch of yours must be runnin' slow. Or perhaps you're losing your grip after all these years. Must be the heat, I suppose, goes straight to your head, see with that old tweed cap still stuck on. Heat can't get out. Look out you don't boil over climbing the hill."

The comic formalities having thus been observed, they proceeded to get down to more serious matters.

"Meeting still on for this evening, then, is it? " Jones the Graves' voice sank to a whisper, which Evans answered under his breath.

"Yes, I'll see you up there as soon as I shut up the pumps."

"All right, see you up there."

And without further exchange, the Graves walked on up the steep street.

These cryptic remarks referred to a proposed rendezvous arranged with the third of the trio who were all at school together in the same class. The last of their generation to survive, and now the oldest inhabitants of the village, their meeting, to be held at the home of Jones the Smallholding, had been kept a closely guarded secret, to be told to no-one.

Now that the appointed evening had arrived, it turned out to be one of those evenings that doesn't seem to grow cooler as the sun sets, and the sullen heat grew heavier as Jones the Graves climbed the cobbles towards Jones the Smallholding's home on the side of the hill, from where it looked down on the village below.

Not a very special village perhaps, just another village like so many others. Yet so strongly had it held and embraced these three old men, who had been born into it, that from week to week, from month to month, year in and year out, they had seldom left this crook of the valley that harboured their homes, tucked in behind the crest of the crag, to shelter, in winter, from the cold west wind.

The one pub, the school, the one shop and the chapel, these were the landmarks of their lives, and each of the three had grown old in the place where he once was young.

Jones the Graves, Jones the Smallholding, and Evans Motors were by now so much a part of the landscape of the valley, that their whole lives were open books in the library of the gentle art of gossip, whose archives ran deep below the still surface of the village's life, to subterranean caves of unfathomable facts and fantastic fictions.

To learn a little of this encyclopaedia of gossip, let us return, for a moment, to Mrs. Williams and Mrs. Owen, still in their sun scorched back gardens. Mrs. Owen was now engaged in prudently hiccuping drops from a galvanised watering can onto her prize pansies, while Mrs. Williams watched over the fence, proffering advice where none was needed.

The two of them were playing a form of verbal tennis peculiar to women of their kind, batting words at one another over the fence as intensely as any game that might be observed on the centre court at Wimbledon.

"Now take Jones the Smallholding," Mrs. Williams opened with a good serve, "there's a fine thing now . . . . I wonder why he never married."

"Living all alone up there on the side of that hill, and never going away as long as I can remember." Mrs. Owen received the service well, and put the ball back neatly in her neighbour's court.

"Always untidy," Mrs. Williams lazily lobbed her return. "Never bothers at all. Always late."

Mrs. Owen rallied: "Never a button on his waistcoat, and never a button done up right on his trousers, either. Talk about fly fishing, I ask you . . . " And she laughed like a drain, so that Mrs. Williams nearly missed her reply.

"Trousers done up with string all the time, and only that old sheepdog for company, other than his chickens, cows, sheep and those goats. If ever there's a man that needed a woman, there's the one."

This reply caught Mrs. Owen's attention wandering, and Mrs. Williams scored a vital point. Both women turned together in silence, to look up through the heat haze at the white-washed stone house: a long low building divided in the middle to separate the human inhabited half from the cattle barn under the same slate roof.

"Could be such a nice house, too," said Mrs. Owen to put the ball back in play. "If only he'd sweep it every once in a while, and not let the goats climb in that kitchen window."

Mrs. Williams received this service well, and came back quick as a flash:

"Oh yes, I remember I went up there for tea once, and nearly got eaten half out of my dress by those goats. They seem to be partial to cotton print. Praps it was the flowers on it."

Mrs. Owen tackled this one easily, coming in with a backhander:

"If I had a pound for every one of them corrugated sheds, I'd be a wealthy woman now, I'll tell you . . . whatever does he keep in them all, I wonder."

At this point something distracted Mrs. Williams and she missed. Jones the Graves came into view, a small figure climbing the distant hillside.

It's deuce. Mrs. Owen to serve.

"Now there's a contrast, Mrs. W." remarked Mrs. O. relishing this opening shot. "There never can have been two men with the same name more different than Jones and Jones."

Mrs. Williams was fighting back, and a swift rally ensued:

"Village never had a better sexton than old Jones. . . "

"He digs a lovely grave."

"Wonder what he's doin' up there this evening . . . "

"Talk over old times, the two of them . . . "

"I suppose so . . . "

Then Mrs. Owen came up with a slam:

"Both of them's going to retire, I hear."

But Mrs. Williams was right on the ball, and came back as quick as a lightening:

"That's right. That's right. And so's old Evans Motors."

This caught Mrs. Owen off balance, and her reply hit the net.

"Is that so? I didn't know that. So all three of them's due to retire."

There was a pause. Advantage Mrs. Williams. She kept up the pressure, things seemed to be going her way.

"Look. There's Evans Motors now."

And sure enough, there he was, in the distance, rolling a little from side to side as he walked, starting the long climb up the hill as Jones the Graves reached the top.

Mrs. Owen was flustered, and she fluffed her return:

"Wonder what they're up to . . . all three of them together . . . up there at the Smallholding's."

Her concentration had gone now, and she was wide open. Mrs. Williams came in for the kill:

"Bet you'd like to be a fly on the wall up there this evening, eh? "

And Mrs. Owen was too busy wondering to think of a reply, so it's game set and match to Mrs. Williams, and the two ladies sauntered inside for tea.

The Meeting

Mr. John Jones' smallholding was a comfortable place, twenty odd acres in small parcels on the hillside. And the man himself was now sat in his rocking chair in the threshold of the front door, around which honeysuckle climbed enthusiastically. Thomas the sheepdog lay stretched on the flagstone floor just inside, trying to keep out of the heat.

His master was whistling through his teeth, a broad shouldered, well muscled man, tanned a deep brown by the sun, his face contentedly lined, his hair greying amid the brown. His shirt was collarless and open at the neck, and his trousers really were done up with string.

He rocked in time to his whistling, as he whittled at a stick with a bone-handed pen-knife. A goat got up from the flower patterned sofa inside, and ambled easily and unhindered out through the door. A tangle of kittens played in a basket under the table. Bundles of drying herbs hung from hooks in the old oak beams. Embers glowed under a black cast iron kettle on a fire of sticks barely alight in the old blackened range. The smell of summer mingled with warm animal scent and wood smoke.

Two days washing up was stacked in the sink. A tap dripped, unhurriedly, into yesterday's beans. The dim interior of the front room contrasted sharply with the fierce brightness of the day outside, even though evening was creeping on.

A fork, a rake, and a hoe leaned against the front door. A small scythe was on the bread board on the kitchen table. A scarecrow, almost completed, bearing strong resemblance to the owner of this property, and indeed wearing his cast-off clothes and hat, sat awaiting some finishing touches, in an armchair that itself needed attention.

In the yard a chicken started up, and ran a few yards, clucking in anger, flapping its wings a few feet from the ground, and Jones the Graves turned the corner of one of the corrugated iron buildings.

The Smallholding continued whistling, though he broke into a grin, and rocked a little faster. Thomas the sheepdog got up and ran to greet the visitor as he crossed the yard, nuzzling against him with easy familiarity.

"Hello, old Tom, boy! " said the Graves, sweating a little after his climb, but still as orderly as ever.

"Evening, the Smallholding! What's that you're doing there, having the day off are you? These farmers are a lazy lot, I must say. "

"Hello yourself. What's wrong with taking the weight off your feet after a day like today? Hot enough for you, is it? ! " The Smallholding picked up the pattern of banter that had grown familiar over the years.

"Look at you now, Jones the Graves, all done up in that collar and tie, I'm surprised you're not strangled in it, in this weather. And you've got your cap on as well! You must be roasted! ! Where's Evans? "

"On his way up now, or should be, though he'll be late for his own funeral, as you know. I stopped by the garage to remind him, though."

"Very good idea. You keep us all to time, don't you, old friend. Cup of tea when he gets here, eh? "

The Graves sat down on an old plank bench under the window, after first carefully brushing it with his hand to remove the cobwebs and dust. Thomas the sheepdog settled at his feet.

"Dry as a desert! Close as hell! You got anything still growin' ? " he remarked, prodding his friend with his elbow.

"Careful, I got a knife in me hand here! You trying to damage me? ! " exclaimed the Smallholding.

"Sorry, I didn't think. What's that you're whittling? "

"A whistle, see, for Megan's boy. Put a pea in it, when its finished. Too damn dry for much to grow."

Their conversation was interrupted by a noise like a demented steam train bursting its boilers. Thomas leapt up, barking ferociously, and Evans Motors, red in the face, forehead running with beads of sweat, rounded the corner of the shed, puffing and blowing like a beached whale.

"Jones, lad, can't you move your house down the hill a bit, it's too much in this weather! ! Look at me, will you, I'm nearly done for after climbin' that lot! "

He subsided onto the bench, next to the Graves, causing the plank to sag dangerously.

"Oh, it's the weight of you that's the problem," laughed the Smallholding. "You know, none of my armchairs will last much longer, it's a crying shame the punishment you hand out to them. Go on, unbutton that waistcoat, there's only the three of us here ..."

"But a meeting is a meeting, eh? " puffed Evans. "We can't all of us afford to be as scruffy as you, Jones the Smallholding, now can we? There is a proper way to do things, you know! "

"Yes, but look at you now! " chuckled the Smallholding. "You may intend to present a picture of decorum, but if you'd of undone your waistcoat coming up that hill you'd be a lot more presentable now, boyo. "

"Oh, leave over you two," The Graves chimed in. "What about that cup of tea you mentioned, or was it my imagination ? We've got some serious talking to you, if you remember. "

"I haven't forgotten the tea or the talking," smiled the Smallholding, as he folded his knife and put it in his pocket. "Kettle should be almost boiled now. I'll brew up."

And he went inside, while the Graves, in wry silence, contemplated the still puffing Motors, who in between wheezes and sighs, alternately grinned, winked, and shook his head.

"Hurry up with that tea! " the Graves called loudly, in mock alarm. "There'll be smoke coming out of his ears in a minute! ! "

The Smallholding, Thomas ever attentive at his bootheels, bustled about within, emerging finally with a tray, holding three more or less clean cups and saucers, a splendid fruit cake, as yet untouched, a large teapot, and a jug of milk.

He handed round the cups, and the Graves discreetly cleaned his with an immaculate handkerchief.

"I'll be mother," Evans offered hopefully, but the Smallholding would have none of it.

"No you won't! ! I'm not having you gorge the whole cake while we're not looking. I'm quite able to pour tea in my own house."

And so he did, and the three of them sat sipping, in silence, looking down in the sunset on the village, the cradle of their days.

There's the slate roofs, slanting grey black above the white-washed walls, and the chimneys with trickles of smoke now oozing out. There's the rusty tin chapel with its little belled tower.

Still there, as on so many days before, there are the streets, terraced along the incline, tarmac black. And there are the trees, neat as ninepins stuck up through the holes in the pavement.

There are all the gates to the gardens, the front doors, some shut, some left open; the windows picked out in favourite colours, and the nameplates marking each owner's choice of a name.

There are the window boxes, some weedy, some tidy; the letter boxes, some brass and some broken; the lamposts climbed and unclimbed, some straight and some crooked.

And each of these streets, this heatwave evening, and each of these alleyways, as the sun sets slowly, is empty of people, as the shadows lengthen.

But to the three old boys on the hillside, each is full of memories of childhood, of schooldays, of work, and of play.

Successes and failures, courtship and mourning, all their comedies and tragedies have been played on this stage, and as they sat there sipping tea, they saw them play again.

"Look, at that! ! There's some clouds coming up! " The Smallholding finally broke into their reverie. "Maybe we'll have some rain! "

"We could certainly do with it! " The Motors nodded, with a mouthful of cake. "It's too hot for me."

The Graves remained silent looking down on the village. Sure enough a bank of black clouds was clearly visible, along the horizon away from the setting sun, which sank slowly towards the crag at the top of the hill.

"Bit of a breeze coming up too," added the Smallholding.

"Damn the weather! " the Graves suddenly snapped. "Let's get on with it. I call this meeting to order. You all know what it's about, but I may as well recap. "

"All right," said the Smallholding. "I'm listening."

"I'll take notes," Evans Motors decided. "It might be of some use later."

"We don't need notes," the Graves shook his head. "It's not that sort of a meeting! "

"I'll take notes just the same, if it's all the same to you, of all the pertinent points."

"Oh very well, do as you please. Now then, as we are all too aware, time does not stand still. I know that we, all three of us, love this village. There's no doubt that it's been a fine place for us. But I, for one, and I know it's the same for you two, am troubled in my mind.

Look here. We've spent all our lives in this one place. We've never seen anything of the world ..."

"Speak for yourself! I went to the Motor Show in London once! " Evans butted in, over the rim of his teacup.

"Do you call that seeing the world? " the Smallholding cut him short. "That's not the point. Let the Graves continue."

"As I was saying," the Graves resumed, leaning forward a little on the bench. "All we've seen is this one little backwater. Oh yes, it's a very pretty little backwater, but it's kept us here all our lives, mesmerised us maybe, so that we've given it everything, and now what, I ask you? What are we faced with in the way of a future,eh?"

He stopped short.

"Retirement," said Evans Motors flatly.

"Retirement," said Jones the Smallholding, equally flatly.

"Retirement! " shouted Jones the Graves.

Then each of them, in turn, exploded, one after the other, shouting:

"The old peoples' home! "

"The geriatric ward! The wheelchair! "

"Second childhood! "

"Decrepitude, decline and decay! "

"Need a magnifier to read the paper! "

"Need a walking stick to creak down to the shop! "

"Losing control! Can't do anything for yourself! ! Humiliating! ! "

"Terrifying! " "Helpless! " "Hopeless! " "Horrible! "

"The End! " "The End! " "The End! "

It seemed they were all agreed, and this outburst was followed by a pause. They sat lost in their thoughts, in silence, for a minute. Then Jones the Smallholding began talking in a rambling monologue that the others nodded in time to.

"I just don't know what I'm going to do with myself when I retire! But it's my sister's boy, see, he's been out of a job these last two years, and he said he was going to emigrate, and it nearly broke his mother's heart to even think of it. So I said, I'm not getting any younger, he can take over the smallholding in a couple of years. Well, now he's gone and got married, and there's a baby on the way, and still, no sign of a job. And the time's up for thinking and talking about it, and I've got to retire.

They've got it all worked out for me to go and live with me sister, but now it's coming close to it, I think I shall go mad with nothing to do. I mean they won't want me coming up here, hanging around the place, and meddling with everything. I don't blame them for that, I'd feel the same.

And if I didn't pass the place on, the Duties would take half of it when I die anyway ..."

"Well, what about my garage, eh? " Evans Motors started up, and took up where his friend left off. "I've spent all my life building up that business, and since my Winnie died the business has been everything to me, 'cept for my boy, David, of course.

But, as you know, he upped and went off to live in the City, and didn't want to know about his old man's firm. Then he changed his mind and came home again, and learned the trade, and now he's damn near as good as me, and it's true, I couldn't manage without him.

But now he says he thinks it's time I retired, and he wants to run things himself, and if I don't give him more control of things, he'll up and go back to town again.

Then what'll I have worked for all this time,eh? Tax'll take it all, if I don't retire, but I don't know what I'll do with myself with no garage to run! What's an Evans Motors worth without any motors, eh? I tell you, I feel like I'm being pushed onto the scrapheap myself! ! "

Jones the Graves could not keep quiet any longer. He stood up, and wagged a finger at his friends, and the village below.

"I've been working year in and year out in this little backwater, for the chapel, for the school, for the council, and now they tell me I'm too old to go on working! Too old! ! I don't feel old! ! I've never felt fitter !

It's true, I've no family business, I've no land, no close family even, since my Gracie died. But I feel just the same as you two about retiring. I know I'm a well respected senior citizen, and I suppose that means they'll put me in a glass case, and gawk at me. But I don't want to be put in mothballs! I won't let them bury me alive! "

"Nor me! " shouted Jones the Smallholding.

"Nor me! " shouted Evans Motors.

Again all three of them sat in silence looking down the hill. The twilight had by now spread all around, making purple with shadows the dim shapes of the trees, and picking out patterns in greys and blacks all across the valley and the surrounding hills.

Along the skyline, still streaked with light, clouds loomed dark over the village below, and the windows of the houses were lit one by one, as lamps were switched on in kitchens and bedrooms, front rooms and halls, sending beams through the gathering gloom. The still air hung heavy and oppressive, as night closed in all around.

Then Evans Motors spoke up.

"I have an idea," he said simply.

"What is it? " said the Graves, equally simply.

"Tell us! " the Smallholding nodded, simplicity itself, still rocking in his chair.

"I propose ..." began Evans Motors, and that was as far as he got, before a clap of thunder boomed above the valley.

Evans Motors rose to the occasion, rose from the bench he was sat on, and as he addressed his friends, he looked positively biblical, a Welsh Moses, about to lead his comrades from the Wilderness.

"I propose," repeated Evans Motors, 'that we do something about it! "

He raised his fist at the threatening sky.

Thomas the sheepdog threw back his head, and let forth a bloodcurdling howl. A healthy breath of wind stirred the trees to sudden motion, and carried the sound of goats bleating down from the crag above.

"Well? ? ! What shall we do? ! " shouted Jones the Smallholding.

"I propose that we set forth on a journey together, the three of us! ! "

A flash of lightning forked through the sky, and another clap of thunder rolled over the village, seeming to second Evans' motion, and he, feeling his moment to have come, continued:

"I propose that we descend from this retreat in these great mountains ..."

"Come off it! " said the Smallholding, but Evans remained undaunted.

"I propose," he shouted towards the oncoming storm, "that we enter the gates of the nearest large town by the shortest possible route. And I further propose that we visit each alehouse in this town or city, in turn, and that, therein, we partake of such liquid refreshment as we may find there, and that we ask of all and sundry that we meet, each and every one of them, no matter how humble or lordly he, or she, may be, that we ask of each one that we meet, what he takes to be the meaning of this life, and how he sees his future. And then may the good Lord have mercy on our souls! ! "

"You mean we go on a pub crawl? ! " Jones the Smallholding was awestruck by the supreme logic of the proposal.

"I do! " replied the Motors.

"A pub crawl! " exclaimed Jones the Graves.

"Precisely," the Motors continued. "A pub crawl of epic proportions. A pub crawl to end all pub crawls! "

"The Last Great Pub Crawl! " shouted the Smallholding.

"The Last Great Pub Crawl! " the others chorused, as the thunder crashed and roared, in seeming approval, and the lightning cut fiery streaks through the sky, slashing the darkness.

Then the rain began to pelt down in a thick and drenching sheet, the sky seemed to burst open, and the three of them stumbled inside the house, to slam the doors, and fasten the windows, to brew more tea, and plan the details of their coming adventure.

Like small boys in the hideout of their secret society, they planned their prank by the light of the hurricane lamp and the fire.

"We mustn't let anyone in on this! " they all agreed.

"It's vital nobody knows! "

"No one outside this room must hear of it! "

"We'll have to keep it a secret! "

"Cross your heart, and swear not to tell a soul! "

"Oh come on, no need of that, surely, Evans! "

On the Wings of the Storm

When, an hour or so later, Evans Motors and Jones the Graves left Jones the Smallholding's house, wrapped in whatever could be improvised in the way of rainwear from old potato sacks and blankets, the storm had still not let up.

The Smallholding stood in the lighted doorway, and watched as the two huddled figures, carrying a lantern aloft, squelched their way across the yard, and into the enveloping darkness.

Clouds scudded across the pale moon, in a night of wild winds. Pale tongues of the great sky serpent forked through the black. Great drums of the booming earth shaker crashed all around.

The two old boys tumbled down the hill. Every trickle of a stream had now become a torrent, suddenly filled; every wheelrut had become a rivulet, every hollow, a pool. The dry, cracked, parched earth turned to frothing mud beneath their feet. Cobwebs in the hedgerows balanced great drops of rain.

Soaked to the skin, they pushed open the lower field gate, and stumbled through onto the cobbled road. When they finally walked into the village, the sound of water was everywhere in the air, running from rooftops, filling empty barrels, splashing from broken gutters onto cars below, and making great puddles in the streets. The rain teamed and gurgled down drains, dripped and dropped into attics and cellars, and rapped at the rattling windows of children whose heads hid under the covers pulled up over their ears.

Flashing ghost light flickered over the horizon, as they made their way past Minnie's shop, where the wellingtons and galoshes hung from their hooks with 'I told you so!' expressions.

"You never do know, now, do you?" had proved true enough, but Mrs. Owen's and Mrs. Williams' woolly whatnots, still hung out on their back garden lines, would not dry out on this particular night.

Inside his jacket, Evans Motors clasped to his breast the notes he had finally made on the planned expedition. Jones the Graves carried the harassed parafin lantern. As they turned into the main street, a sudden stillness was followed by a deafening crash, as the storm hung directly overhead.

Evans Motors slipped on a curbstone, and bumped heavily into Jones, who flew forwards, but kept on his feet. The unfortunate Evans, however, fell flat on his back, lost his grip on his papers, and his precious notes were carried aloft by an unrepentant wind.

"My notes! My notes! " he cried. But Jones was indifferent to their fate.

"Come on, Evans, you great buffoon, they're no use anyhow. I told you that from the start! " he yelled, as he pulled the bedraggled and cursing Motors to his feet.

They stumbled arm in arm the rest of the way to the garage, where they said their storm-lashed goodnights. And Jones the Graves walked the last of his journey home alone.

Each of them, on getting indoors, immediately made ready for bed, armed with hot water bottles, warm drinks and extra bedclothes. And both of them fell quickly and soundly asleep, thoroughly exhausted, but excited in their hearts.

Outside the storm reeled and staggered on its way round the sleeping village. The wind made sport with Evans' notes for most of the night, dispersing them far and wide.

One vital page, however, written, as they all were, in the garage proprietor's unmistakable hand, with his mechanic's indelible pen, on the garage bill pad he had used as a jotter, was carried by some freak of fate, into Mrs. Owen's back garden, where it became entangled with her washing line.

When, with the dawn, calm returned and the storm abated, there it was, this bedraggled piece of paper, clinging, together with the wet and woolly wild vest and drawers, to the limp and dangly line.

The sun tiptoed quietly around, as if trying to apologise for the uproar of the night before, and doing its best to dry things out as well as it could. Understandably, the village scene was a little pale and watercoloured, this bright morning.

Mrs. Owen rose at eight, as usual, and had her usual breakfast, of tea, toast, and two lightly boiled eggs. Next door, Mrs. Williams was also up, in her kitchen that was the mirror image of her neighbour's, where she ate an identical breakfast, except that her eggs were hard boiled.

Both ladies looked out of their kitchen windows, as they rinsed their dishes at their symetrical sinks, and took pity on the washing, on their parallel lines, deciding it would be better to dry it indoors, as the weather was so uncertain. Would it scorch or drench today?

"You never do know, now, do you? " Mrs. Owen remarked over the fence, after the customary exchange of identical good mornings between the two ladies, in their side by side gardens.

After taking down her pegged out particulars, and carefully wringing them out over the rose beds, Mrs. Owen noticed the unusual extra item that had attached itself to her line. She viewed it for some seconds with considerable distaste, before her natural curiosity got the better of her.

"What's that then? " Mrs. Williams queried, over the fence.

"Don't know yet, do I? " Mrs. Owen replied, and the morning match had begun, with her at an unfair advantage.

"Piece of paper, by the look of it, blown in by the storm? "

"Let's see now, oh yes, it's on Evans' Garage notepad paper, and that's Evans' handwriting, too, look."

"Somebody's bill is it? What's it say, can you read it? "

"Not sure if I should ..." Mrs. Owen hesitated, more for theatrical effect, than from any real prickings of conscience.

"Oh, go on! " Mrs. Williams urged her. "Can't do any harm."

"Well I don't know ..." Mrs. Owen was savouring the suspense, but then she herself could no longer resist.

"Let's see now ... oh ... that's odd, that's very odd, I don't know what to make of this! "

"Let me see! Let me read it! " Mrs. Williams was becoming quite agitated, but her neighbour was by now engrossed in the scrawl.

"No, no, I'll read it aloud! " she announced finally, and then she proceeded to do so.

"Minutes of the Meeting of the Three. Jones, Evans and Jones present," she read.

"Oooh, fancy that, well I never! " Mrs. Williams chortled. "So that's what they were up to up there! A meeting, eh? I wonder what on earth for? ! "

"Will you give over? ! " Mrs. Owen rebuked her. "I'm trying to read this. It's not that clear ... let me see ... yes ... here we are ... it says;

'It is proposed that, considering the inevitability of the dread state of retirement being forced on us three, who have done nothing to deserve it, we must do something as a gesture of defiance against these ungodly pressures, and as a protest against the relentless flow of time.'"

"Well I never," Mrs. Williams chortled again. "So that's it, is it! ? That Evans always one with the words! "

"Will you give over? ! " Mrs. Owen was obliged to repeat. "I'm trying to read the rest of it ... there's a big blotch, then it says:

'... we hereby resolve that on the first Saturday in September of this year, we shall leave this village, in the late afternoon, departing from the garage of Evan Motors, and proceeding to set out on a journey, in the school bus belonging to the firm of that name; and that we shall, in the aforementioned vehicle, drive to the nearest large town, that being Hereford; and that there we shall proceed from one pub to another, enquiring of all and sundry that

we meet, as to their understanding of the meaning of this life, which we three, despite our alleged antiquity, are quite at a loss to understand in the circumstances we find ourselves in.

It is further resolved that this proposed undertaking, or Quest, be known as 'The Last Great Pub Crawl', and that it shall be kept a closely guarded secret to be told to no one."'

"Well I never! Well I never! " Mrs. Williams positively crowed with fascination. "Whoever would have thought it! ! I mean those three old boys are the pillars of the community! Chapel elders! Well I never! "

And Mrs. Owen, too, was quite carried away.

"Fancy this getting stuck on my line eh? ! Must of got blowed away in the wind last night. So that's what they were up to! ! "

"They don't want to retire then, that's it! " concluded Mrs. Williams intelligently.

"Silly old fools! " laughed Mrs. Owen, fondly. "There's a time for that, for everyone! "

Gareth Powell, the newsboy delivering the morning papers, followed by Milko Davies, on his rounds, and Bert the Post, on his, were soon informed of the extraordinary news, each one, of course, with a stern admonition to keep it to themselves.

But before elevenses, half the village knew of it, and by lunchtime Minnie the Shop had a sore throat from telling all her customers, and she had to close up for an hour to enable her to recover down at the pub, which was itself alive with conversations on just this one topic.

The telephone exchange was busier than it had ever been before, and all afternoon the switchboard was jammed. Calls went out to outlying farms, over the far side of the valley, and by tea time, the news had even reached distant relations in places like Cardiff, Llandrindod Wells and Aberystwyth.

There was much discussion over supper that night, of what was to be done, though Evans, Jones and Jones knew of none of it, as the news that their adventure was known about was a better kept secret than the original secret itself. The three continued with their plans, in great and growing excitement, unsuspecting that their every move was carefully observed, and was the subject of much speculation all over the valley.

Neither the odd wink of the eye behind their backs, the few rather strange, oblique, comic remarks at the petrol pumps, nor the odd cryptic exchange over the graveyard wall, or at chapel after the service, led the three old boys to believe that their secret was out. They were too busy themselves, winking at each other, behind the backs of those whom they believed did not know of their plans.

The Great Day Dawns

By the time the appointed day arrived, the village was a hotbed of rumour and counter rumour. But Evans, Jones and Jones still lived in blissful ignorance. Everyone had, at every turn, dutifully played out the charade of nothing out of the ordinary being afoot.

It was the same on the great day itself.

Evans rose as usual, and opened the garage his usual five minutes late. Jones the Graves performed his morning's duties with his customary punctuality, and high on the hillside, Jones the Smallholding could be observed, at work in his fields in his usually casual manner.

All over the village, lunch was gobbled behind closed doors, as the excitement mounted. There was a distinct buzz in the air, but it could just have been the change from Summer to Autumn.

As the afternoon wore on, however, the strain of secrecy was beginning to show, and there was some evidence of bad temper here and there, like the nerves before a first night.

Children were snapped at by normally breezy fathers; husbands were hen-pecked by customarily cooing wives; grandmothers scolded, kettles boiled over, fires went out by mistake, and refused to relight. Dogs got the odd kick for no reason, cats were cuffed off the cushions of armchairs that were usually theirs by right, and doors were closed with a little more of a bang than would have seemed normally necessary.

Round about tea time the suspense was getting unbearable. But then, Jones the Smallholding was spotted, sneaking down the hill in his sunday best , which meant he was only slightly less untidy than usual, shooing back the goats which insisted on following him all the way down to the field gate.

The news of his descent spread like wildfire, by the jungle telegraph of whispers and subdued murmurs.

Then Jones the Graves was seen, walking in a peculiarly nonchalant manner towards Evans' Garage, as if he was just out for a stroll. He looked even more immaculately turned out than usual, which meant that his boots and buttons positively shone, and his trousers had creases that looked as if they might cut you. He had his very special cap on his head, and as he ducked in the back door of Evans' Garage, he sighed with relief, thinking himself unnoticed.

He was followed shortly afterwards by Jones the Smallholding, who also considered himself very fortunate not to have met anyone in the street. This very lack of any encounter or even a near miss, should have aroused their suspicions, but they put it down to luck and good timing on their part, confident they were unobserved, and carried along by their excitement.

Within a minute, Evans Motors himself had joined them, sneaking across the yard from his bungalow, and into the dim echoey interior of the big garage building that housed the school bus and the breakdown truck

"Everything go according to plan? " Evans whispered, squeezing in through the small back door of the garage, and sliding it to after him.

He looked more than usually dapper, and his shiny new boots squeaked a little in the hushed building, as he tip-toed over to the others beside the bus.

"Went like a dream! " whispered Jones the Smallholding.

"Like a treat! " whispered the Graves.

"Very good! " Evans Motors continued, still whispering. "As Transport Manager, I propose that we embark without further ado, and simply put our foot down and try to make a quick getaway. Agreed? "

"Agreed! "

"Agreed! " came the whispers from the two Joneses.

"Righto. I, of course, shall drive," Evans went on, "Jones the Graves will navigate, and Jones the Smallholding, you will stand by to open all doors of buildings, gates, and so forth. Agreed? "

"Agreed! "

"Agreed! "

"All aboard then, and let's go! ! " Evans concluded.

And without further ado, they all piled into the school bus, which could not by any stretch of the imagination be described as modern, but which might politely be referred to as of classic vintage, though that would be rather a flattering description for a vehicle that had given thirty years good service.

Evans climbed up behind the big steering wheel, put the key in the ignition, checked that his passengers were safely aboard, and pulled the starter.

There was a whir, and a click, and a cough, then nothing at all. Evans grimaced.

"Try her again," he said, and he did so.

This time a strange hubub emerged from the engine such as a completely inebriated orchestra might produce if asked to improvise on the theme of mechanical failure.

"Can't think what's the matter ... I checked her over very thoroughly yesterday, and she was running as sweet as anything! "

"Any petrol in her? " whispered the Smallholding, from the running board, where he was standing waiting to open the garage doors when the engine started.

"Course there's petrol in her, what do you think I am, stark, raving mad? ! " hissed Evans, and he tried the starter again.

The engine let forth a long drawn-out sigh, and was silent.

"Damn and blast! ! " shouted the Motors, forgetting to whisper, and the two Joneses both shushed him, with fingers to their lips.

"We'll have to go in the breakdown truck, nothing else for it! " Evans announced, in an outraged whisper.

"Come on, then! " said the Smallholding, and the others climbed down to join him, and walk stealthily over to the even more ancient breakdown truck. This vehicle had all the dignity of its age, and indeed looked rather awesome, resembling nothing so much as an old battleship that had survived many years at sea.

"Does it still go? " whispered Jones the Graves, in wonder.

"What do you mean, does it still go? ! " replied Evans. "Of course it still goes! This thing would climb Everest, if it had to! ! "

"Never mind Everest, will it get us to Hereford and back? "

"Course it will! " Evans was optimistic, but not without reason. "Do breakdown trucks break down? Whoever heard of such an idea? ! "

Evans, and the Graves climbed aboard. The truck started, with a roar of choke, at first go, and Evans inched it forward towards the big garage doors, which Jones the Smallholding was poised ready to open.

But, at the sound of the engine firing, something very strange indeed happened. The garage doors swung open from the outside, without Jones the Smallholding touching them, and as the three old boys eyes adjusted from the dim interior of the garage to the bright afternoon sunlight outside, an astonishing sight met their bewildered gaze.

As the breakdown truck crept slowly forward, it became apparent that in the garage forecourt was gathered every single inhabitant of the entire village. Young and old alike, they stood in neat rows, waving and cheering.

Not since the Coronation had the village put on such a gala display. The brass band, drawn up in ranks in full uniform, began playing a rousing march to which the male voice choir sang along with great gusto. A large banner, with 'LONG LIVE THE LAST GREAT PUB CRAWL' embroidered on it, in flowers, was held aloft on two poles by Mrs. Owen and Mrs. Williams, one at each end. The overall noise was overwhelming after the whispered hush within the building.

"What in heaven's name! " Evans Motors exclaimed.

"How on earth did they find out? ! " Jones the Smallholding was flabbergasted.

Jones the Graves just gasped.

There was no way through the assembled multitude, so that, for several minutes, three red-faced elderly Welsh gentlemen were obliged to sit crammed inside an antique breakdown truck, in their best clothes, feeling extremely ridiculous.

Finally, Evans Motors began to laugh, quietly at first, but then in a great crescendo of mirth that threatened to burst the breakdown truck at the seams, as the other two joined in.

The village school children ran forward, scattering confetti and streamers, as a multi-coloured batch of balloons rose silently towards the clear sky, and in what looked remarkably like a pre-arranged drill manoeuvre, a gap appeared in the massed ranks of villagers, making a path through the crowd.

Evans shifted into gear, and the truck moved slowly into the street through the assembled throng of smiling humanity.

Once clear of the forecourt, Evans put his foot down, and the truck lumbered away, gathering speed, flanked on each side by two laughing leather clad motor cycle outriders, two of the village ton-up boys. They stayed alongside, until the truck passed the 'End of Speed Limit' sign, where the houses stopped, and the hedges of the countryside began. Here the motor cycles pulled up, turned around, and one Evans, and two Joneses, grinned sheepishly at each other, as they rumbled on down the valley towards the main road to Hereford, leaving a cloud of dust rising from the road behind them, such as might be raised by a division of tanks in the desert.

Brief Journey

Several miles passed by, without a word being spoken, and the three old men sat watching the countryside roll by in silence. The rattle and clank of truck's lifting gear, and the healthy roar of its engine, would have made conversation a considerable effort, requiring plenty of volume.

Telegraph poles flashed by. Farms, glimpsed over hedges, were closely scrutinised by Jones the Smallholding for signs of good or bad husbandry. They slowed down almost to a standstill climbing steep hills, holding their breath till they made it to the top, with queues of frustrated saloon cars fuming behind, unable to overtake. Then, after a quick glimpse of the spread of the landscape from the hilltop, they rattled down the other side at breakneck speed, making up for lost time.

They steadied to a fair cruising speed on the stretches between hills, where the saloon cars took turns to overtake, each driver taking his heart in his mouth, like a kamikaze pilot, as he passed the lumbering giant of a truck on the narrow winding road.

The rain that had followed the drought had brought a richer green back to some of the fields, which now were every imaginable shade and hue, from the full spectrum of greens, to brown, through yellow, even going as far as purple.

They idled the engine through several small villages, before turning onto the main road, from where it was a steady run all the way.

Signs of excitement were beginning to show: the drumming of fingers on the dashboard here, the tapping of the toe of a well-shined boot there, the straightening of a tie that did not need straightening, the delicate adjustment of the angle of the peak of a cap.

Jones the Smallholding was the first to speak, raising his voice above the mechanical clamour.

"That was quite a send-off, eh? Nearly brought a tear to my eye!!"

"Certainly was quite a turn out! " shouted Evans, from behind the wheel.

"Where are we making for, when we get into town? " piped up Jones the Graves, a great one for thinking ahead. "Where have we decided to start? "

"I reckon we should make for the Cattle Market," said Jones the Smallholding. "Hereford's a big place, but I know the Cattle Market, and the Market Tavern's just next door to it. I've been there before, and it's as good a place to start as any."

"You bin there before? " queried Evans, at the top of his voice. "That must have been before the war! " he laughed. "Do you reckon its still there after all these years? "

"Look here, Evans," the Smallholding shouted back. "You mind who you're talking to, now. You don't know everything there is to know about me, you know. Same trouble with you as with all the rest of the people in that village. Think a feller's never been any other way than he is now. People can change, you know, if other people will let them. 'Course I bin to Hereford a few times, but I don't make a big fuss about it, not like some people I could mention, with their bragging constantly of their one trip to London to visit the Motor Show! "

"All right, all right! Keep your hair on! " Evans yelled, as he swung round a wide bend. Passing a grey stone church on one side, and a hotel on the other, they drove through a village cut in half by the main road.

"Well, you know what I mean," continued the Smallholding, "That's just what we're trying to get away from, that narrow way of looking at things. No point in setting off for wider horizons, and pastures new, carrying all the same old guff with us, now is there? "

"All right, all right, I was only joking! I apologise. There's no need to fly off the handle! " Evans complained.

"He's right though," shouted Jones the Graves. "If we want to fulfil the purpose of this adventure, we must keep our eyes and ears open. If we're going to get anything out this at all, we must be ready anf willing to experience new things! That's the way of the future.

It won't be easy. But it's no good looking backwards. We must all agree to leave behind our preconceptions about each other, and about other people, else we might as well stay at home in the village, and retire like good boys, without going making nuisances of ourselves asking 'what's it all been for? ' Is that agreed? "

"Agreed! "

"Agreed! "

The other two shouted their assent.

"They won't get me retiring without a murmur! " the Smallholding yelled, as they came to the top of a long hill, from where they could see the road sweeping ahead of them in a broad descending curve. Beyond that, way below, lay the grey smudge of the city, with smoke rising, into the late afternoon sky, from the factory chimneys.

"Look! There she is! !" shouted Evans.

"I can see the Cathedral! !" the Graves shouted back.

"Look out, Hereford, here we come! !" sang out the Smallholding.

And five miles farther on, the old breakdown truck whizzed past a forty mile an hour limit sign, followed rapidly by a sign that said 'Welcome to the City of Hereford'.

A few minutes later, driving slowly and sedately now, they entered the outskirts of the town, and were surrounded by the rows of identical houses in a typical modern estate.

The sun was low on the horizon. The evening, and the town, lay before them.

Part Two
The City

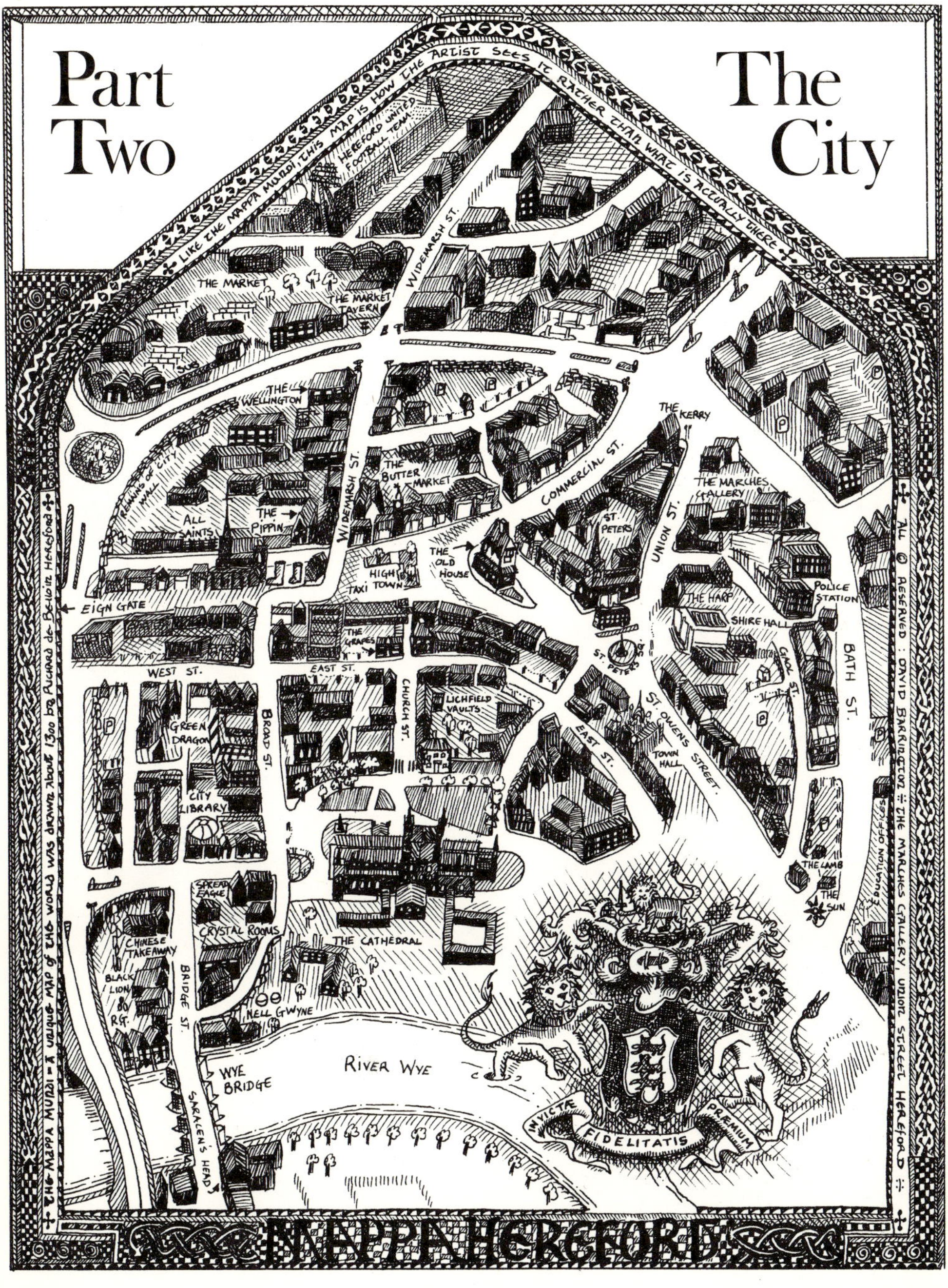

Market Tavern

Lost and Found

"Which way do we go? ! " shouted Evans, as they approached a roundabout, and pulled up at the dotted white line in the road. "Jones the Graves, you're supposed to be navigating. Which way is it? "

Signposts pointed the way to various other towns, which was not much help. Some young lads stood at the kerb, waiting to cross the road. They were fascinated by the breakdown truck and had undoubtedly never seen anything like it before. They were trying to guess its age and make.

"Which way to the town centre! " shouted Jones the Graves, his head pushed out of the window. 'We're looking for the Cattle Market! "

The lads laughèd among themselves, nudging each other and giggling. Finally one of them spoke up and gave some directions, with a cheeky grin.

"Second left out of this roundabout, and over the new bridge. Then, after a second set of traffic lights you come to another roundabout. Go into this roundabout and take the second left out again. Cattle Market's just there on your left! "

"Got that? " Evans hissed to Jones the Graves, as the cars behind began to hoot.

"Got it." The Graves nodded. "Thank you! " he shouted out of the window to the Lads on the kerb.

And the old truck nosed its way forward into the traffic. They took the right turning out of this first roundabout, but somehow or other confusion crept in at the second one, which resulted in their circling round and round several times before deciding which way to go.

"Which road is it, then? "

"I don't know, they all look alike to me! "

"Oh come on now, don't exaggerate ..."

"Well, which way did they say to go? "

"Second left, they said."

"Let's try this one."

"No, no! That's the one we came in on. Can't be that one! "

"What about this one, then? "

"All right, let's try it! "

And they turned off into the wrong road, which led them half way round the town, and down by the railway station. They had to ask directions of two further groups of pedestrians before finally they pulled into the car park beside the Cattle Market. They piled out of the vehicle, locked the doors, dusted themselves down, straightened themselves up, and took stock of their situation.

"Well, here we are then," Jones the Smallholding observed.

The big modern buildings of the Cattle Market were closed up, and the cattle pens were empty of animals. The Market was deserted and a little forlorn, like an abandoned stage.

The last straggles of football supporters made their way towards the town in twos and threes, with nowhere in particular to go, and late returning shoppers bustled the other way, after having tea in town when the shops had closed an hour or so earlier. Cars hummed by in both directions down the dual carriageway of the busy ring road, some going home after a busy day's work, others bringing in the first of the evening's cinemagoers or a party of people on the way to a restaurant. There was the beginning of a Saturday night buzz of expectancy in the air.

"Yes. Here we are, as you say ..." echoed Evans Motors distantly, as he surveyed the scene.

"Come along then. Let's find the first pub." Jones the Graves was the first to pull himself together, and he turned to the other two. "Are you fit? " he asked.

"I'm fit! " said the Smallholding.

"Lead the way! " said the Motors. "To the Market Tavern, boys! "

And three abreast, smart as sailors disembarking on shore leave, they walked towards the pub of that name, which stood close by, set back a little from the edge of the ring road.

A smart Georgian building, recently painted, small striped canvas awnings over some of its windows, and with a new pub sign on a post outside, the Market Tavern, surrounded by the benches and bollards of its concreted car park, looked a promising proposition, a good place to start.

"It's still here then, eh Evans, old boy," Jones the Smallholding teased, nudging his friend in his not inconsiderable midriff, as they jostled in through the brass-handled, glass-paned door. "I'm not as green as I'm cabbage looking, you know, they've just painted it up a bit that's all. It hasn't vanished, see ..."

But just inside the door he stopped in his tracks, and the others cannoned into him from behind.

"Good God! " he exclaimed. "Whatever have they done to the place! ! "

Loud music blasted out into the tiled lobby they were standing in. Straight ahead of them were some louvred Western-styled cowboy saloon swing doors. Jones the Smallholding approached these warily, followed, a step or two behind, by his two friends. The steel tips on the heels of their boots chinked on the tiled floor, for all the world like outlaws fresh into town.

The Smallholding peered over the top of the western doors into the bar beyond, with a look of blank amazement on his face.

"Good God! ! " was all he could think of to say.

On a small stage at the far end, a trio of youths strapped into guitars were chewing up the air with a Country and Western song, singing, here in the heart of Hereford, in suitable cowboy drawls, something about being ".. busted flat in Baton Rouge, and waiting in the rain ..."

"What's the matter? " enquired Jones the Graves. He was stuck behind the other two, and was neither tall enough to see over the Smallholding's shoulder nor able to see anything at all past the rounded frame of Evans.

"Nothing's the matter," rumbled the Smallholding. "It's just that this place used to be so different. They've tarted it all up. There used to be sawdust on the floor in there, and just a plain and simple room. It was a real farmer's pub. But look at it now! "

And he made way for Jones the Graves, who pushed in through the swing doors, followed by his friends. The doors, and the decor within had a very pronounced effect on Evans, who swaggered a little as he walked across the room, as if he had just dismounted, and tied his horse to the post outside.

Western waggon wheels hung on the walls, alongside an odd looking cork substance, also for a Western effect, not altogether successfully achieved. The bar itself was constructed of large ranch house beams, and one might easily imagine oneself on the set of an Italian B. Movie, soon to be ravaged by a bloody gunfight between a cigar-chewing villain and his blue-eyed adversary.

Evans, by now, had the gleam of a successful bank robber in his eye, although the two Joneses still seemed somewhat overpowered by the place, and were looking nervously around at the handful of customers sat at the wooden tables or standing at the bar. Evans attempted to break in on their thoughts, by the most direct means possible.

"How about getting a drink in, eh? What'll you have. I'll buy the first round to get us off to a good start. What are you having? "

But they didn't seem to hear him.

"Come along now, you two! ! " he said, as he took them each by an arm, becoming Marshall Evans leading his suspects to the bar. "I seem to remember you lot spouting about being open to new experiences. Well how about me offering to buy the first round, isn't that a new enough experience? " Then his voice dropped to a whisper. "Hey, look at that barmaid, will you! ! "

This last remark seemed finally to bring the others back into focus, and they followed Evans' gaze to the young lady behind the bar. She proved well worth looking at, a bosomy big-eyed blonde, with an engaging smile.

The band stopped playing, and there was a sudden space of silence. Evans leapt into it, waving to the barmaid, and shouting genially in her general direction.

"Good evening, my dear! You have here before you three strangers to this town from over the border, badly in need of liquid refreshment after a journey of some miles, and equally thirsty for knowledge, or information, leading perhaps to a new perspective on life. We wonder if you can help us? ! "

To her credit the barmaid neither blushed, nor baulked, at this unusual opening from this portly Welsh gentleman. Indeed, she continued to smile her engaging smile, and replied in a pleasantly matter-of-fact English country girl's voice:

"Well. Let's start with your drinks, and see where we go from there, eh? "

"Make it three pints of best bitter, if you please, my dear," said Evans. "And may I say how pretty you are? "

"That's very nice of you to say so, I'm sure," said the barmaid. "Three pints of best bitter coming up! ! "

And she turned and reached down three glasses from the shelf behind her, giving, without realising it, a fleeting glimpse of a cute derriere.

"Do we have to check our guns at the bar? " enquired Jones the Smallholding, with a wry smile, as she turned back to face them again, and began pulling at the pumps. She smiled, and winked, and said no.

"She makes a grand picture, eh? Look at her at those pumps will you now, lads! ! " exclaimed Jones the Graves, and then, always the gentleman, he asked:

"Will you have a drink with us? "

"Don't mind if I do, love," she replied, still smiling. "I'll have a gin and tonic, if that's all right. Thank you very much."

The drinks dutifully paid for, and the change duly counted out, Evans Motors resumed his enquiries.

"Do you believe there's a purpose to all the seemingly random events we have come to know as day-to-day life? Do you know your goal and destination at all? Have you a dream or ambition? "

"Or are you a ship, all at sea, with no maps, like the three of us you see before you? " chipped in Jones the Smallholding.

The singsong Welsh lilt of their voices was peculiarly infectious and subtly melodic. The barmaid had to pause for a while to gather her thoughts, and during this pause she served two packets of crisps to a couple of blue-denimed lads who had drifted over from a table by the stage. The band struck up again, and the girl behind the bar had to shout.

"Well," she began. "I believe there's a serious note in what you're saying, although you're making a joke of it all. But I don't think you're taking the mickey, so here goes. I'll just say whatever comes into my head."

"Good girl! " Evans Motors shouted, nodding encouragement.

"I seem to just live from day to day," she went on. "It's not a bad life, if you don't ask too much of it. I believe in myself, and I've got some good friends, though there's not many I'd say I could turn to if I really needed some help. But I like to stand on my own two feet and be independent anyway. That's why I've got this job. I don't just want to get married, and fill a house up with kids. I want to see a bit of the world before I decide when and where I'll settle down."

"Well said! " chimed the Smallholding. "That's just how I feel! "

"Girl after my own heart! " Evans Motors exclaimed. "I knew it the minute I first set eyes on her."

"But what about the future? " Jones the Graves wanted to know. "Don't you want a little security, something to rely on? "

She pursed her lips, rang the till for another customer's pint, dispensed change, and smiled her smile again.

"Well, I look at it this way: there's nothing certain in this world. It might all end tomorrow with a big bang, or I might get knocked down by a bus. I just keep going as best as I can, and try to have some fun on the way. Where are you gentlemen from, did you say? "

"Oh, nowhere in particular," Evans answered, gulping at his pint. "Just a little old village over the border into Wales. But that's just it, don't let's talk about us! We want to find out what's been going on out in the big wide world, all these years we've been stuck away up there in the middle of nowhere."

"We are pilgrims, if you like," said Jones the Graves, solemnly, expressing his ecclesiastical bent. "In search of some answers to infinite questions."

"We're on a pub crawl," added Jones the Smallholding, down to earth as ever. "It's to be known as 'The Last Great Pub Crawl', and yours is the very first pub."

This definitely caught the blonde girl's interest.

"Really? That's wonderful. It sounds really exciting! Can anyone join you? I'm off duty in ten minutes, I only had to stand in for the first couple of hours tonight, for a friend who wanted to visit her mum this afternoon, and couldn't get back in time. I've nothing to do this evening. I was only going to watch telly, but it sounds like it might be much more fun to join you! "

"It certainly should be more entertaining than watching the telly. We'd be delighted if you'd come along." Jones the Graves' chest swelled with chivalrous pride, as he accepted on behalf of his friends, and then turned to them for confirmation, which came at once.

"Evans Motors, at your service, my dear, and we'll be glad to have you aboard," said the gentleman of that name.

"Jones the Smallholding," said the other Welshman. "Glad to make your acquaintance. You'll be able to show us the town. We've already got lost once, on our way in, in the motor."

"Oh well, I know Hereford like the back of my hand," said the barmaid. "My name's Victoria. And don't none of you make any wisecracks about stations! I didn't choose the name, but I've learned to live with it, provided I don't have to hear the same joke every time I'm introduced! "

"Victoria is a very elegant name," said Jones the Graves seriously; one might even be tempted to say gravely.

"And might I say it suits the young lady," added Evans Motors.

"Very queenly," smiled Jones the Smallholding, into the bottom of his beer mug.

"Oh no! " sighed Victoria, feigning a mock swoon. "That's another prize chestnut I could live without hearing again. It won't be long now till I'm off, but how about another pint, while you're waiting? "

Quoits and Questions

And so it was, that the three who entered the Market Tavern stone cold sober, left a little later with a couple of pints each inside them, and a pretty girl to guide them.

They stopped in the now darkening street to discuss which pub to go to next and then, without having reached a decision, they carefully crossed over the dual carriageway, pausing in the middle to wait for a gap in the traffic, before dashing over to the other side of the road.

"There's the Farmers' Club," remarked Jones the Smallholding. "I've been there a few times, in my younger days."

"Come on, this pub'll do, won't it? " said Evans, nosily looking in through the half curtained windows of the Victorian brick building on the corner of Widemarsh Street. "This looks all right to me. The Wellington."

"No jokes about boots now! " said Victoria, smiling at the Smallholding.

"What have they got in there? " asked the Graves, not tall enough to see in himself. Evans obliged him with a commentary on the scene within.

"Looks like a sporting sort of pub to me. There's lots of flags on the wall behind the bar. Hereford United mostly, I think. They've got a one arm bandit. And this could be just the job if you fancy a game of darts, or quoits. What do you think, Victoria? Seems fairly quiet ... not too crowded."

"Well, there's a lot of pubs in Hereford, but this one's okay," she replied.

"You don't drink here yourself, though, I suppose, what with only working over the road. So what other pubs are there? " asked Jones the Graves.

"Let me see now," said Victoria, laughing. "There's the Bowling Green, The Tabard, the Booth Hall Hotel, the Castle Pool, the Golden Fleece, the Golden Lion, the Black Lion, the Lichfield Vaults, the Orange Tree, the David Garrick, the Brewer's Arms, the Bricklayer's Arms, the Oxford Arms ..."

"We've got a real expert here, boys! " Evans Motors interrupted, but Victoria was not easily put off.

"Then there's the Grapes, the Greyhound Dog, the Saracen's Head, the Plough, the Racehorse ..."

It seemed the list was inexhaustible, but Jones the Graves butted in, laughing.

"Stop, stop! That's enough! You're making my head turn round! "

"Oh come on! Let's just go in here, and give this Wellington place a try, seeing as how we're here. I fancy a game of quoits! " said Jones the Smallholding, already holding the door open for the lady of the party to enter first.

"And I fancy another pint, it's my round I believe," said Jones the Graves. "Same again for everyone, is it? " He received three affirmative answers, and made straight for the bar. The others made for the quoits board.

The few customers already in this pub looked up at the purposeful entrance of these newcomers, and watched as an intense match began. Jones the Graves carefully carried the drinks over, without spilling a drop, and set them down on a small table.

"Good shot! " the Smallholding shouted, as Victoria scored a quick twenty points. A large, smartly dressed, silver haired man, in a business suit, stood close by at the bar.

"Funny things we get up to, eh? " he said, slowly and deliberately, in a broad Yorkshire accent. "Tossing little rubber rings at a nail stuck in a bit of board, and scoring points for it! Pretty odd sort of thing for grown men and women to be doing, though, ain't it? "

"Just a bit of fun," beamed Evans Motors, over the rim of his glass, which he then raised in a toast. "Here's to the spirit of fun! Long may it reign! " And the others all raised their glasses, including the Yorkshireman.

"Spirit of fun! ! "

"I'll drink to that! ! "

"Cheers! ! "

The stranger then opened the conversation again.

"I've nothing against the spirit of fun, mind. Though I don't hold with rowdyism, and I draw the line at these soccer hooligans ..." This was obviously the beginning of a set piece speech, of an extremely boring nature, which Jones the Smallholding anticipated and fended off neatly, with a well-timed interruption of perfect simplicity.

"You're from Yorkshire, aren't you? " he said, with an expression of complete innocence. Evans Motors, who was standing next to him, quoit in hand, paused before his next shot, and cast an admiring glance at his friend.

"Cunning old fox," he thought to himself.

The stranger swallowed the red herring, without noticing it, and introduced himself.

"Aye, lad, happen I am. Stanley Hoxton's the name. I'm in town here on business, and I stopped over for t'football."

The others introduced themselves, the game of quoits continued, and Jones the Graves politely enquired:

"What line of business are you in, then, if you don't mind me asking? "

"Ask away, lad! " said Stanely Hoxton, in expansive mood. "I'm in plastics, this is the age of plastics: there's a great future in plastics, that's what I always say."

A cheer rose from Evans and Victoria, drowning this conversation for a moment. And there was a mock boo from Jones the Smallholding, as Jones the Graves missed the board completely, so intent was he on what Stanley Hoxton was saying. The quoit had landed, with a splash, in a pint mug on the table.

"Look what you're doing, Jones the Graves, boy, or you'll drown us all! " yelled the Smallholding.

"Good job it's his own pint," Victoria added, with a laugh.

"Play fair! " teased Evans Motors. "No cheating now, just 'cos you're not winning! "

Jones the Graves good naturedly retrieved the quoit from his pint, took a long pull from the glass, licked his lips, and sighed.

"That's better. Not a bad drop at all. Sorry you lot, my concentration was slipping, talking to this gentleman here. He say's he's in the plastics business."

"Plastics, eh? Very twentieth century, too," said Evans, coming over to Mr. Hoxton. "Salesman for a big firm are you? "

"I *am* a big firm." said Mr. Hoxton, swelling visibly. "Hoxton's Plastics and Extrusions International Incorporated. Chairman and Managing Director: Stanley H. Hoxton."

This momentous piece of information brought the game of quoits to a standstill. There was a moment's silence. Mr. Hoxton stood where he was, savouring the effect of his words. Then he raised his glass of whiskey to his lips and, pointing his nose at the ceiling, emptied it in one gulp.

"Hoxton's ... Plastics ... and Extrusions ... International Incorporated ... That's quite a mouthful," said Victoria, running her tongue round the words as she spoke. "I would imagine, Mr. Hoxton, that you started at the bottom, made the long climb to the top the hard way, and that you are, in short, a self-made man! "

Stanley Hoxton lowered his glass slowly, and looked at Victoria as if noticing her for the first time.

"That's right! " he said. "How did you know? " He seemed genuinely surprised.

"I just guessed," she replied. "You seem to fit the part."

"Smart lass. You're not just another dumb blonde, after all. I suppose you've second sight, eh? "

"Maybe," said Victoria.

"Well, come to think of it, happen it's plain enough. I suppose I am a bit of a stereotype. I forget that business isn't everything, sometimes, and I get carried away with meself. Plastics isn't everything, but it does mean a lot to me. Even though I'm not ashamed of me background, and me lack of any formal education, like, I suppose I do go on about the firm and how successful it is, to cover up. Over compensating, that's what they call it, I believe. But I did make good with all the cards against me at the start, it's true, and that is important to me. I didn't mean to throw it in your faces, though, and I do apologise. Er, excuse me ..."

Mr. Hoxton now seemed to have rather upset himself, and he turned towards the bar as if about to leave. It seemed something needed to be said, and Jones the Smallholding rose admirably to the occasion, in his usual no nonsense manner, coming out with one short sentence.

"We're on a pub crawl," he said quietly.

Mr. Hoxton turned back towards the group round the quoits board, as the words hung in the smoke filled bar.

"The Last Great Pub Crawl," said Evans Motors mysteriously, and a flicker of a smile twitched at the corner of Mr. Stanely Hoxton's lips.

This was enough of a signal, and in a rush, all talking at once, the idea of, the purpose of, and the particular point reach in the adventure, were explained to the at first bewildered, then interested, and finally, enthusiastic, Chairman and Managing Director of Hoxton's Plastics and Extrusions International Incorporated.

"What was that toast? " he exclaimed.

"To the spirit of fun! " they chorused.

"I'll join you! " he shouted, and they drank the toast again.

Victoria Tours

At the end of the game of quoits they left the Wellington, and the company of the night's quest had swelled to five. They stood outside the pub for a few moments, on the corner opposite the Farmers' Club, tossing quips, instead of quoits, at one another. Then they walked down Widemarsh Street towards the centre of town, feeling contentedly merry.

"Lead on MacDuff! " roared Evans Motors, at nobody in particular.

"No one by that name here! " Jones the Smallholding answered, as the ring of Welsh boots sang on the pavement.

"I feel quite outnumbered, the only girl here, with all you men! " laughed Victoria. "You sound like a lot of bother boys! "

"What are they? " asked Jones the Graves.

"Hooligans! " said Stanley Hoxton.

"Where are we going now? " asked Jones the Smallholding, quickly fending off the possibility of Hoxton sounding off on that subject.

"Victoria! You're supposed to be our guide! " shouted Jones the Graves. "Will you be so good as to tell us where we are going? "

"Very well," she replied. "Let's see now." And she assumed a tour guide's voice, cupping her hands to form an imaginary megaphone. "On the left, straight ahead of you, gentlemen, you will see the Gate of India Restaurant, while here on this side of the road, you will notice an excellent shop selling fine china of every description. And what a magnificent display you see before you, here in the window: cups, saucers, bowls, teapots, and indeed ornaments of every shape and pattern."

"I feel a bit like a bull in a china shop, tonight, I can tell you," joked Evans Motors.

"A Hereford bull! Ho! Ho! " quipped Stanley Hoxton, laughing at his own joke.

"And now," continued Victoria, in the guided tour operator's voice she was to resume at intervals throughout the evening. "Allow me to direct your attention to this fine specimen of a brass plate, marking the door of the Hereford County Liberal Club! "

"Vote Liberal! " shouted Jones the Smallholding. "The only sane party! Far too long out of power! "

"Rubbish! " shouted back Evans Motors. "Labour, every time! "

"Never! " yelled Jones the Graves. "Any sensible person would vote Conservative! "

"Quite right! Encourage free enterprise! That's the true spirit of Great Britain! Keep Britain great! " boomed Stanley Hoxton, in his broad Yorkshire.

"And as we pass on to the next shop, Gentlemen," Victoria went on, "please note the fine wickerwork and the interesting decorative household items displayed for sale. You are kindly requested not to discuss politics, at this stage of the proceedings, as brawling on the public pavement is not encouraged by Victoria Tours.

Over to the left you will see the elegant mock Tudor facade of the shoeshop on the corner, at the rear of the famous Butter Market. This mock Tudor theme is again picked up by the next building, here on our side of the road. This hostelry, known as the Imperial, enjoys a reputation with those visitors to the City who wish to dine out of an evening. In other words, it's a pub you can eat in! Shall we go in? Is anyone hungry? "

A quick discussion, followed by a show of hands, revealed that no one felt like eating. And a look through the door convinced one and all that they might safely pass by this pub, on this particular evening.

"Bit posh for me, I think," said Jones the Smallholding. He had, by now, removed his tie, and his shirt collar looked as if it would not be long in following. So the company passed on down the street, not wishing to make any of their number feel ill at ease.

"Guns, ammunition, hardware, ironmongery, tools and bathroom equipment; all under one roof, here on your right, Gentlemen," announced Victoria Tours, through the imaginary megaphone, as they passed the next shop. "While over on the left hand side of the road, you will observe the side entrance of the Butter Market, and the offices and showrooms of the illustrious Midlands Electricity Board, praise the Lord! "

This remark brought them to the door of the next pub.

Strange Brew

The Pippin is an unpretentious place, with an easy welcome. It has a sort of shop window onto Widemarsh Street, through which the drinkers in the front bar can both see, and be seen. Anyone passing by the corner of the alleyway that leads down behind All Saint's Church, can tell at once what sort of pub this is, and the five pub crawl participants pushed on in through the door of the third pub of the night, without pausing for further discussion. The landlord was himself serving behind the bar, and he looked up as the door clanged to behind them.

"Evening Gentlemen. Evening Madam," he said with a smile. "Be with you in a moment." His greeting was returned by one and all, and he finished off serving a young couple at the bar.

"Now then, what'll it be? " he asked.

"Three pints of best bitter, one large whiskey, and what'll you have Victoria? " Stanley Hoxton ordered, loud and clear, ending with a question thrown in the young lady's direction.

"Make mine a Pimm's, with a slice of lemon, please." replied Victoria.

"Well, that's different! " said Jones the Graves. 'I've never heard of one of those."

"Well you must try one, then, Jones! " said Stanley Hoxton. But the Graves was uncertain.

"The spirit of fun, remember," teased the Yorkshireman.

"Well, I don't know." Jones the Graves still wavered.

"Come on, open yourself to new experiences, and all that, remember? " Evans Motors reminded him.

At this point Stanley Hoxton took over.

Market Tavern
THE LAST
GREAT
PUB CRAWL
Saracen's Head
A REALITY CRISIS
Black Lion

Wellington
The Pippin
CITY OF HEREFORD
Site of the birthplace of
NELL GWYNNE
Founder of
CHELSEA HOSPITAL
& mother of first
DUKE OF ST. ALBANS
born 1650
died 1691
The Grapes Tavern
Lichfield Vaults
Bar

"Er, landlord, would you kindly cancel the order for whiskey, and the pints of bitter, and if it's not too much trouble, we would appreciate a large bottle of Pimm's and five glasses. A lemon cut in slices, and an orange, ditto, would be most welcome, if you have them. Thank you."

Stanley Hoxton was nothing if not precise when ordering. Obviously, he was a man who knew what he wanted, and it would appear, he usually got it. The landlord disappeared for a minute, and then returned with the bottle requested.

"You're in luck," he said. "I don't usually stock this, but someone ordered a bottle a while back, and never called for it."

And he laid it on the counter, as his wife came through a door with the orange and lemon slices. Stanley Hoxton paid with a crisp fiver, the drinks were duly poured, and various toasts were exchanged.

"Cheers! "

"Cheers! "

"Present Company! "

"Absent friends! "

"Bottoms up! "

The three Welshmen raised their glasses tentatively to their lips and sipped, at first in a gingerly manner. But then the drinks disappeared quickly enough.

"Quite an interesting taste," said Jones the Smallholding, licking his lips.

"I love it! " said Victoria.

"Not bad at all! " said Evans Motors.

"Not sure," said Jones the Graves.

"Try another drop," offered Stanley Hoxton. "Lots of new drinks to try yet ... all part of the night ..."

"Well, maybe I will try another," said Jones the Graves, his reluctance diminishing noticeably.

"Don't mind if I do! " said the Smallholding, and the glasses were refilled all round.

"This time the toast must be 'The Last Great Pub Crawl! '" shouted Victoria.

"What's that? " asked the landlord, and they told him.

"Have a drink! " invited Stanley Hoxton, now truly in generous mood. The landlord accepted, glasses were raised, and this further toast was duly drunk.

Music drifted in through the door that led to the other bar at the back.

"Jukebox is it? " asked Jones the Graves. His natural impish look was by now much enhanced, and there was a mischievous rake to the angle of the peak of his cap. Jones the Smallholding's shirt collar had joined his tie, tucked away in a trouser pocket, and Evans' waistcoat was unbuttoning, button by button.

"No, it's not the jukebox," said the landlord. "We have a folk club here in the cellar bar on some nights. It's usually on a Tuesday, but it's on tonight instead this week. It's very pleasant. You can take your drinks down there, if you like."

"Folk club is it? That'd be all singing, and so on, I suppose," said Jones the Smallholding, turning to the others. 'Sounds interesting, eh? "

"Lot of longhaired hooligans, and layabouts," sniffed Stanley Hoxton.

"Oh come on, now," chided Victoria. 'Keep an open mind, Stanley. I think it would be a great idea to go down there! "

"I'm very fond of music," said Jones the Graves.

"Very well, let's go then! " exclaimed Evans Motors, revving himself up off the stool he had perched his not inconsiderable bulk upon.

Music

With the landlord leading the way, they trooped out into the back bar, and from there they clattered down the winding stone steps, to the cellar bar below.

"Loos are down here, as well! " remarked Evans Motors, with a laugh.

"That's handy," added the Graves, as they turned a corner and descended the last two steps, going down through some old oak panelled doors, and into the dim, smoky club.

A short, friendly looking, bearded young man greeted them from behind a table, just inside the door.

"Evening. Fifty pence, please," he said, seeming a little surprised at the age of the gentlemen in the party.

"Fifty pence? ! " queried Evans Motors. "That's ten bob in my language! Is that for each of us? "

"'Fraid so," said the young man on the door.

"That's quite normal these days," Victoria pointed out.

"Damned inflation! " muttered Stanley Hoxton.

"I'll pay," offered Jones the Graves.

"No, I will," said Jones the Smallholding, firmly. "It's my round."

"Fair do's," said Evans.

The Smallholding paid for their admission, and in they went, jostling their way down, through the crowd, to the bar at the far end of the first of two vaulted stone rooms. One might say that the effect was one of being beneath some great castle, perhaps in the dungeons, or the wine cellars. This first room, lined along the walls with wooden benches pulled up to large wooden tables, was linked to the second room by a low archway, about six feet wide, through which the sound of guitars and voices now came, loud enough to be heard above the general level of conversation.

Stanley Hoxton placed the bottle of Pimm's on the bar, and glasses were refilled or topped up, as appropriate. The song that had been in progress since they entered, came to an end, and there was a flurry of applause.

Looking through the archway, they could see that the young man who had taken the money at the door, was now standing at the microphone. He cleared his throat.

"Evening, everybody, and welcome to the Cellar Folk Club once again," he said. "We try to encourage floor singers here, so I'd like to introduce a young man from Ireland, who I've never met before. He's just on his way through town, it seems, and tonight he's going to play a few tunes and sing something for you, before he travels on again tomorrow. So, a warm welcome please, for Michael O'Donahue! "

During the applause that followed, Stanley Hoxton shouted: "What's a floor singer then? ", and Victoria just had time to shout back: "Someone who sings from the floor of course! ", before the sound of a penny whistle, clean, sharp and clear, cut through the thick air of the club, playing a jig.

The place went absolutely quiet. Then the audience began to tap their feet, or bang their knuckles on the tables, quietly, in time to the music. As the quick-silver sound wove its spell around them, it changed all the time, moving along, now fast, now slow, now sad, now gay, bringing to mind memories perhaps long buried, a friend's face, or a forgotten dream.

The tune danced on, now like the sun on a waterfall, now like a butterfly flitting through a forest, now shrill, like the sharp call of a bird. It exulted, and lamented, somehow calling forth the feeling of a past age, and a green landscape of scattered cottages, peopled, after dark, with leprechauns in the starlight.

The music rose in volume, filling the two rooms, and its rhythm grew firm. As it did so, the gentle toe tapping of the crowd became a banging of glasses and fists on tables, till a few people began to rise from their seats, and dance, arm in arm around the floor, laughing and bumping into one another, spinning round and round, as best as they could, in the confined space of the crowd. The jig became a reel, and the reel became another jig, until, when the music ended, there was a great roar of approval and a great clapping of hands, and a stamping of feet for more.

Evans, Jones and Jones, Victoria and Stanley H., craning their necks to see into the other room where the music had come from, could just make out a tall, tousled haired, fine featured, young man with blue eyes, and an ear-ring in one ear. He was dressed in an old pin-striped suit, that looked as if it had come from a jumble sale, and he stood smiling at the response to his music. A spotlight, that usually shone on a dartboard on one wall, was now turned to light the area that served as a stage. It appeared to be shining rather in Michael O'Donahue's eyes. When the uproar subsided, he spoke in a broad Irish brogue, not very loudly, and rather shyly.

"I'd like, now, for to sing you a song that I wrote the words of meself, to a traditional fiddle tune. It goes something like this:"

He cupped his right hand to his right ear, closed his eyes tightly, tilted back his head, thrust out his chest and drawing a deep breath, he began to sing, a slow, solemn lament, that broke in great waves of sadness over the hushed room. His singing voice was quite different to the one in which he had spoken, altogether more confident, and sure of the notes:

"I am a stranger now,
in my home town.
I've travelled this whole country round,
and all this country o'er,
but in my hour of coming home,
I found strangers at the door.

And when I asked them
where my mother and my father
might presently reside,
I was told that, long ago,
both of them had died.

The evening it was coming in,
and night was close at hand,
I walked up the street,
unto the Church,
and in the graveyard
I did stand.

There in the growing dusk,
plain for me to see,
was the stone that marked
the resting place,
of those that gave birth to me.

Why did I stay away so long,
why did I so long tarry,
only to find,
on coming home at last,
my dear ones dead and buried ?

I walked through the twilight streets,
that I had known so well
as a child,
and though the town had changed
in many ways,
yet there remained
much that was the same,
even after all that while.

It cheered my heart a little
for to see
the schoolyard where I used to play,
bringing to my mind
the happier time
of my childhood days.

Then I came unto the house
where my sweetheart used to dwell.
I stood outside the door, in the dark,
and rang upon the bell.
When the door was opened
it grieved me sore to learn,
that my childhood love
had gone away
never to return.

Why did I stay away so long
why did I so long tarry,
only to find,
on coming home at last,
my love's gone away
and married.

I am a stranger now,
in my home town,
this place will hold
me no more.
I cannot stay another day
there's nothing to stay for.

I shall be a wanderer,
and the road shall be
my home.
From this day forth,
until I die,
I shall forever roam."

Memories

When Michael O'Donahue's song ended, the last note remained hanging in the air. There was a full minute's silence before the applause thundered out all around the room, with whistles and shouts for more coming from every side. But the young Irishman said a quick, shy, 'thank you', and ducked out of the spotlight, through the archway, making a beeline for the bar.

As he pushed his way through the crowd, the club organiser's voice could be heard, above the continuing cries for an encore, thanking him for singing and introducing the next artists, who began to sing a country and western flavoured song, accompanied by a couple of guitars.

Michael O'Donahue reached the bar, and found a gap between the thin Jones the Graves, and the stout Evans Motors. He called out to the barman for a pint of Guinness.

"Let me buy you that," said Evans, clapping him on the back. "That was fine singing and playing, if I may say so."

"Very fine indeed," added Stanley Hoxton.

"Oh, it was nothin' at all! But thank you very much just the same," said Michael O'Donahue, looking as if his escape routes had been cut off, surrounded as he was by these elderly strangers. But then Victoria spoke up and Michael's expression changed to a grin, as if the cavalry had arrived in the nick of time, for a last minute rescue.

"I liked your song," she said. "And I think the story it tells is true. Am I right? "

"You are," replied Michael. "How did you know? "

"The girl's got second sight," said Stanley Hoxton, remembering his own earlier experience of Victoria's quick grasp of his character.

"Oh no, nothing like that at all! " laughed Victoria. "It's just that you sounded so much as if you meant it. As if you had lived it in fact."

"One pint of Guinness," interrupted the barman. Michael took the offered glass, and Evans paid for it.

Evans, Jones, Jones, Hoxton and Victoria had by this time consumed all but the last few drops of the bottle of Pimm's, and while they were by no means the worse for the drinks, it would be fair to say that their already fertile imaginations were by now well watered, and their tongues somewhat loosened. Michael O'Donahue buried his nose in the creamy head of his Guinness.

"Oh, it's fine to get a jar down," he said. "Even if it's not the real thing, and only out of a bottle! "

"No draught down here, eh? " nodded Stanley Hoxton.

Jones the Smallholding had been silent for a while. He now spoke quietly in his sing-song Welsh way.

"You know that thing you were playing, that whistle or pipe or whatever it is ... it really took me away for a while ... It took me right back to my childhood, and I remembered clearly what my mother looked like. I saw her, just as if she was standing right here in this room. Bringing the cows in, we were, and I was just a lad again, in the buttercup and daisy days gone by. I just want to say thank you. That really meant something to me."

"Not at all, not at all," Michael O'Donahue replied. "It's my pleasure, I'm sure. I'm glad you enjoyed it."

He seemed to feel more comfortable now and to be enjoying the company in general, and Victoria's in particular. Evans Motors tapped him on the shoulder.

"It's a funny thing, though," he said. "But while you were playing I remembered my first car! Now there was a sight! " This remark made everyone fall about laughing.

"From the sublime to the ridiculous, in one giant step! " said Jones the Smallholding.

"Oh, you can scoff," Evans continued. "But although I've had dozens and dozens of cars since that first one, as you know, that particular car was very important to my development. It was a crucial event in my life buying it, I can tell you. I'd saved for months and months, putting by every penny I could, and keeping all the money in a tin under my mattress. I counted it so often, I swear the notes was half worn away by the time I had enough put by."

The picture this conjured up was the cue for more laughter from the others, but it didn't stop Evans telling his story.

"An old Austin Seven, she was," he went on. "And I swear she had a personality all of her own. If you didn't talk to her nice and proper, and flatter her a bit besides, she wouldn't go at all!

Well, she was pretty tatty when I first got her, of course, what with not paying that much for her, but I soon put her to rights, and then I was the proudest lad in the village, and the only one with his own car. I took all the girls about in it, I did, going for spins around the valley with these other two, here, along for the ride, as often as not.

And what with all the kissing and cuddling going on in the back seat, it was a right carry on, I can tell you. Quite a cause for concern, I was, to the Chapel Elders, a real tearaway, and ne'er do well, and a corrupting influence on the morals of all I took out in that car, which was branded as an instrument of the Devil in a fiery sermon one Sunday. And after that, all the girls wanted to ride in it, of course, but their mums were not so keen on the idea. I was considered rather a bad lot, you see.

But now look at me! I'm a Chapel Elder myself, a respected businessman and a Councillor to boot, about to be forced into an early grave by a premature retirement that will make me dull as dirt! "

"Oh come on, Evans," said Jones the Graves, who was the first to be able to control his laughter enough to be able to speak. "You always were a bit of a lad, and you always will be, however much you try to be a good steady fellow. Listen, I'll tell you though, do you know what I thought, while he was playing that whistle? "

The chorus of no's, and the shaking of heads encouraged him to continue.

"Well, I'll tell you," he said. "Though it's sad enough I'm sure. Being the village sexton, I've seen a lot of funerals, and the like, you know, and my two friends here, Jones the Smallholding and Evans, are the only ones left from the class we were in together at school. All the others are dead. If the two wars didn't get them, something else did. But while he was playing his whistle, I was back in that old schoolroom in the village, and we were children again, running around, laughing and playing, with our whole lives stretched before us. And it felt very strange, when the music stopped, to know we're at the other end of the line now, and it's all behind us, and not wanting to face up to what we know comes next, or maybe a bit afraid of it ..."

His voice trailed off, but Stanley Hoxton was quick to get his oar in next.

"That is very sad, true enough," he said. "But look here, I'm a practical man, and with me there's always something to be done. You can't give up, just because you're getting old. I mean, I'm no chicken any more myself. My business has been my life, and I can understand how you feel about retirement. But there's lots of hobbies you can take up, lots of interests you can pursue, courses you can study, even. Think of all the things you've longed to do but never been able to do, because you never had the money or the time. While he played his whistle, I saw my whole business grow all over again, in fast motion, and I understood quite clearly how work is its own reward. You can't say you've wasted your time, you know."

Michael O'Donahue had been listening attentively to all that was said. Now he finished his Guinness and remarked: "It seems that my music has taken you all back into your various pasts, and that's all very well and good. But there is another thread there that weaves into the future, you know. There's always something just up around the bend, though you never do know what it is, till it's here."

"But that's just it! " exclaimed Jones the Smallholding. "When you get old there's only the past; we don't seem to have much of a future. That's why we set out on this pub crawl! "

"Pub crawl? " asked Michael O'Donahue. "What's all this about a pub crawl? "

"That's it," laughed Victoria. "The pub crawl! ! That's what I was thinking about while you played. I was looking at your eyes, and wondering what you were thinking, and wondering what you would make of The Last Great Pub Crawl! "

"For the love of God," Michael pleaded, "will somebody please tell me what all this is about? "

"It seems," said Victoria, still laughing, "that The Last Great Pub Crawl is a journey into the future, searching infinities of empty space for a glimpse of truth. And I think you should join us! "

After some further explanation, less poetic but more practical, the proposal was agreed to, and Michael O'Donahue joined the company, bringing his instruments with him. They finished their drinks and climbed back up the stone stairs from the Cellar Folk Club, where the music continued.

Incident in High Town

"Where to next? " asked Stanley Hoxton, and a general hubbub of questions, counter questions, and answers, rose into the warm night air from the street corner outside the Pippin. Then Victoria held up her hands for silence. The hubbub subsided, and she reassumed her previous role of guide to the City of Hereford.

"Never fear, Gentlemen," she announced. "Victoria Tours offer a comprehensive service to cater for the visitor's every need. If you will kindly step this way, we will approach the town centre."

And the five men followed the young lady across the little alleyway to the place where the narrowed end of Widemarsh Street opened out, to the left, into a wide, well-lit pedestrianised open space, surrounded by shops. Dotted around, here and there, were little groups of park benches. Brick bordered flower beds sprouted late summer shrubs and ornamental trees, and a queue of taxis stood, idling, by a phone on a pole.

"This elegant piazza, square, or precinct," intoned Victoria, into her imaginary megaphone, "is known as High Town. It was recently resurfaced, at considerable expense, with its pleasing paving slabs and interesting patterns of brick cobbles.

At the far end you will observe the beautiful Tudor form of the Old House, being all that remains of the former half-timbered glories of this City, which was once entirely constructed in such materials. Now, if you would care to turn this way, Gentlemen, and look back beyond the other end of the pedestrian precinct, you will observe the large modern shop premises at the far end, on the left. You will notice, in the top corner, another much smaller fragment of this style of building, embedded in among the plate glass and concrete, at second floor level, by order of the planning authorities."

And sure enough, they could plainly see a little gabled and timbered house-top, with leaded windows, somehow perched in the front of the modern building.

"Looks bloody ridiculous, stuck up there," remarked Stanley Hoxton. "Waste of bloody money. I like the Old House, though."

Evans Motors had a curious look on his face. He squinted back towards the particular planners' quirk under discussion.

"I haven't had that much to drink yet! " he muttered. "But that Church spire, back there, seems to be bent all to one side! "

The others followed his gaze. Silhouetted against the night sky, there certainly was a decidedly unstraight looking spire.

"That," said Victoria, "is not a hallucination engendered by the intake of alcoholic beverages. It is indeed the famous spire of All Saints' Church, which has a graceful curve in its perpendicular.

But may I now direct your attention, Gentlemen, over this way, and ask you, for the present, to ignore the numerous invitingly lit windows of the big chain stores, the supermarkets, boutiques, jewellers, tobacconists, butchers, bakers and banks. I would like you to consider, for a moment, the building here before you, known as the Butter Market. This is indeed an interesting facade, with, as you see, a Victorian clock tower, adorned with a cupola and bell. And below the clock, above the entrance, you will, no doubt, note the fine statuary.

The Butter Market within is known for its many excellent stalls, particularly those selling fresh vegetables, and the other county produce grown by local worthies. The market is in many ways a focal point in the community, as was expressed in a booklet by a well known poet, who lives locally."

"These bloody poets! " Stanley Hoxton interrupted. "I've never known one that couldn't make a mountain out of a molehill, and there's many of them can hardly speak the Queen's English, if I'm any judge! "

"Never mind the Queen's English, boyo," said Evans Motors. "It's the Welsh that's the true bardic tongue, and that's for certain! Home rule for Wales! "

This was greeted by murmurs of approval from the two Joneses, but Michael O'Donahue would have none of it.

"Oh, come on now," he said affably. "There's many a fine Irish poet, and the old ballads of Ireland will stand as long as there's anyone left to sing them! "

"Well, that may not be too long, at the rate you lot are killing each other off over there," retorted Stanley Hoxton bluntly. "Where's the poetry in that? "

They were all standing in a group in the centre of the open space of High Town, and the discussion seemed to be veering rapidly towards an argument. Michael O'Donahue positively bristled.

"That's a typical Englishman's narrow-minded attitude," he said, with strong feeling.

"And that's a typical belligerent Irishman's attitude," replied Stanley Hoxton, with equal conviction.

"Now hold on a minute," said Jones the Smallholding, trying to calm things down. "There's no call for us to fall out over national boundaries."

But there were still rumbles of dissent from the Irishman and the Yorkshireman. Then Evans Motors, as agilely as his well-rounded bulk would allow, jumped up onto the seat of a conveniently sited bench, from where, surveying the faces of the five others, and the general scene before him, he seemed to be about to deliver an oration.

The sight of him, poised thus, with his thumbs thrust into the armholes of his bulging, half unbuttoned waistcoat, was enough to restore some measure of good humour, and the others could not long keep from laughing, as he huffed and puffed, and hummed and ha'ed, in his pose as the parliamentary windbag.

"I, Gareth Gwyn Evans, also known as Evans Motors," he shouted, raising his voice to the rooftops, and causing a few pigeons to fly up in alarm. "Being a garage proprietor, and person of otherwise good standing, at present under sentence of immediate retirement, hereby declare this to be a public meeting, and roving open debate, in which all and sundry are cordially invited to participate. All those in favour say 'Aye'."

A chorus of 'Ayes' was followed by catcalls, and spurious applause. The one taxi driver remaining at the rank looked nervously over in their direction.

"I therefore declare this meeting to be open! And may God bless her, and all who sail in her! " concluded Evans. And as he got down from the bench, Jones the Graves, still remarkably neatly attired, climbed up to speak. He matched his old friend in eloquent nonsense.

"I hereby propose, second and vote myself in, as chairman, secretary, treasurer and committee, and in these capacities I declare that, in the event of the breakdown of other democratic processes, the Marquess of Queensbury's rules shall apply.

Furthermore, there shall be no slanging, mud slinging, or cursing in front of the ladies. No use of foreign languages is permitted; no blunt objects are to be wielded, or caused to fly, in a manner liable to provoke a breach of anything whatsoever; no unfair advantage is to be obtained by means of subterfuge or wily arts of an oriental nature. Lastly, I offer to buy the next round in the next pub! "

With these words, he, in turn, stepped down from the bench to be replaced by Stanley Hoxton, who looked around for a full half minute, with a serious expression on his face, before speaking. Quite a number of passersby had been attracted by the interesting and oddly comic spectacle presented by the previous speakers, and a fair-sized crowd of all ages and types of people had now gathered.

A raggedy older woman, in a drab raincoat, with a weather-beaten face and greying hair plaited in a pigtail, stood with several large bundles at her feet. She heckled in a marvellously mellow deep-toned voice, that rang with resonances of woodsmoke and cider apple orchards.

"Cooer, look at this 'un up thar! Looks a fair treat dun'ee? Give us a speech then Napoleon, ducks! "

Something about Hoxton's serious expression rendered him even more comic than the previous speakers. A couple of long-haired lads, who had just joined the crowd, now added to the verbal assault, shouting:

"Come on, Gaffer, spout it out! "

"Lay it on us, your lordship! "

"Tell it like it is baby! "

"Get it on! "

Stanley Hoxton spoke with the firmness and dignity of one who has found his platform, and is determined to have his say. His broad Yorkshire tones rolled around the open space, and silenced the uproar.

"The trouble with this country today," he bellowed, "is plain as the nose on your face. Yet the causes of this trouble are ignored and allowed to flourish! There is too much state interference in every sector of life. The blundering nationalisation of every inefficient concern that cannot survive in the fierce competitiveness of today's world markets, leads directly to the crippling taxation that is being imposed on every business that does make a profit, by hard work and initiative under extremely difficult circumstances.

From the big corporation, right down to the small trader in his corner store, the story is the same: one of rising overheads, increased costs and diminishing returns. And, as if that were not enough, the red tape of the bureaucrats further hampers those with the pluck to struggle on.

We've all seen the vast office complexes built to glorify the status of those who are, or should be, the servants of the public, not its masters. And where does the money come from for these, and the other follies of our ever-expanding government departments? I'll tell you: the money comes out of the pockets of those that work to make the nation pay its way.

And this same hard-working silent majority, who are all that remains of the spirit that won the last war, are obliged, nay compelled, to support the thousands of loafers, scroungers and layabouts that sponge along on the dole, abusing a system created to relieve the real suffering of the genuinely needy ..."

Stanley Hoxton had really gone over the top with this last remark, and it seemed he had tried the patience of the crowd too far. A barrage of heckling ensued.

"Self-righteous old windbag! " the lady with the weather-beaten face and pigtail shouted.

"Capitalist pig! " someone else added. "Reactionary old bastard! "

To his credit, Stanley Hoxton knew enough not to outstay his welcome and with one last passing shout about having struck a blow for common sense and freedom, he stepped manfully down from the bench and into the still swelling crowd. One of the long-haired lads jumped up to take his place.

"Freedom? " he shouted. "There's no such thing in this repressive society! ! You're all so hemmed in by repressive social conventions, you wouldn't know freedom if it came and kicked you up the backside! What sort of a life does your average man have? Working nine to five, a five-day week, not enough in the wage packet at the end of it to even think of ever getting off the treadmill of his rent, or mortgage, and his H.P. payments!

Oh, yes, I've worked in the factories! You get to be like a battery chicken after a while! Peck a pellet in one end and an egg comes out the other! I know, I've done it myself. But now I'm out of it, and I tell you I'll never go back.

We've all been brainwashed by the TV, to think we need all these consumer goodies, all this junk, all this hire purchase stuff, that falls apart before you've even paid for it, all these instant quick-as-a-flash foods that contain no nourishment, made in factories for factory-made minds!

It's all a con, a big trap! Get your slice of the good life, trample on the weak, rape the planet's resources, and be better off than your neighbour! Mortgage your soul! Sell your birthright!

No, if you want to talk about freedom, you've got to stop swallowing all the stuff the system pumps out at you through the TV every day. The system's just designed to perpetuate itself and keep those on top on top. You've got to see things for yourself, educate yourself, and I don't mean the kind of education you get in college. That's just programming you for a slot in the machine.

You see, all this talk about work is all very well, but that's not all there is to life! Man's got to expand himself to fulfil his potential! You've got to be an outlaw to be free in this day and age. And if there is no freedom, then there always will be war! "

The young man climbed down, amid a mixture of cheers and boos, and red in the face with excitement, he rejoined his friend. The crowd seethed with lively debate between the two extremes of point of view thus far expressed, eagerly awaiting the next new development.

This proved to be something of a surprise. The lady with the pigtail dumped her bundles and half climbed, half was hoisted, up onto the bench.

She made a quaint figure in her ill-assorted collection of clothes. A fine silk scarf, tied round her neck, clashed both in colour and in tone with the baggy raincoat that enfolded her like a tent. Below the bottom of the raincoat, the hem of a long bright flowery-patterned dress hung, as if in defiance of the upper layer's lack of colour. Her brown muscular legs ended in a pair of clogs, covered in mud. She was, in all, a fine and striking woman, despite her unusual attire, and as she raised her face to the crowd, a gold ear-ring glinted on each ear. Her clear blue eyes looked straight ahead. She said nothing at all. She stood quite still. A hushed and expectant silence fell over the crowd.

Then she began to sing. Her voice had the rough and ready, unschooled charm of someone who had sung for pleasure all her life, and to whom singing was as unselfconscious a reflex as walking or talking. In the act of singing she became childlike, a strange waif of a girl again, vulnerable and yet with a strength and power, beneath the fragile surface, that seemed ancient.

The song she sang, and the way she sang it, immediately created a sense of fun, and releasing the tension in the crowd, brought smiles back to the faces of one and all, after the serious turn events had taken. The tune was very simple and rather like 'The Farmer's in his Dell', repeating itself around a simple refrain. Evans Motors, the two Joneses and Victoria, were hemmed in by the crowd against the bench, and they joined in with the singing as soon as they got the hang of it. Even Stanley Hoxton joined in at the end of the first verse. Michael O'Donahue had picked up the tune with his pipe, from the very beginning, for although no one had heard the song before, it seemed strangely familiar.

"An' if you know a man,
an' if you know a man,
an' if you know a man
that is a thatcher by his trade,

please send him up my way,
please send him up my way:
for me roof is leakin' full of holes,
an' the water's comin' in,
an' if I don't find a thatcher soon,
I shall have to learn to swim!

An' if you know a man,
an' if you know a man,
an' if you know a man
that is a tinker by his trade,
please send him up my way,
please send him up my way:
for me pots and pans are knocked about,
me kettle's nearly lost its spout,
me barn's tin roof is all wore out,

an' if I don't find a tinker soon,
I'll go mad without a doubt!

An' if you know a man,
an' if you know a man,
an' if you know a man
that is a carpenter by trade,
please send him up my way,
please send him up my way:
for me kitchen shelves have fallen down,
me crocks an' cups lie all around,
me chairs are shaky, me stairs are creaky,
me bed's only got three legs, an' I'll be bound,
if I don't find a carpenter soon,
the whole house will come tumbling down!"

The verses continued wryly through the whole spectrum of possible men whose trades might be pressed into service, to save the lady from the greatest imaginable variety of calamitous collapses that were said to be about to occur to the fabric and structure of her existence. As the song progressed, it became more and outrageously absurd. The baker, the butcher, the banker, and many more were drawn in to it by some ingenious twist of its own peculiar logic.

The general mirth the song created remained when it ended. A spontaneous cheer arose from the crowd, which the old lady acknowledged with a deep bow, and a shower of blown kisses. Then she stepped down from the bench, ending up next to Jones the Smallholding in the close crush of the crowd. Such was the festive spirit that now prevailed, that he embraced her enthusiastically and shouted to her how much he had enjoyed the song. She beamed at him, and thanked him.

Evans Motors had meanwhile clambered back onto the bench, and inflating himself to his largest possible size, he roared out over the din:

"I propose that this meeting be hereby adjourned to the nearest pub. 'The Last Great Pub Crawl' is open to one and all! Anyone wishing to continue this exploration of the wonders of the night, along with us, may do so, entirely at their own peril!"

"Victoria, lead on! Where's the next port of call?" asked Jones the Graves, a small man, all at sea in a large crowd.

A fight appeared to have broken out somewhere at the back, between two roving bands of the supporters of the rival football teams that had been playing in town that afternoon. Strange gutteral chants, mostly indecipherable to the uninitiated, rose above the general fracas. But 'We are the aggro boys!' repeated to a pattern of handclaps, was clearly distinguishable, and depressingly familiar. This would have been enough to have served as a warning to anyone who had had the dubious privilege of witnessing this primitive tribal ritual before. Evans Motors had, however, never encountered this big city phenomenon, and he stood still, head and shoulders above all those around him, on the bench looking out into the jostling Saturday night crowd.

"Peace, Peace, he is not sleeping! " he began to sing, in mock operatic tones. A bottle whizzed past his ear, but he didn't seem to notice it. He continued in a melodramatic voice: "Let Nation speak Peace unto Nation! ! " An empty tin can flew through the air. This time it caught him squarely on the side of the head, and bounced off. He recoiled in disarray, and yelled:

"You bunch of mangy nincompoops! Who do you think you are? You're just the sort who spoil the fun for everyone! "

He was answered by cries from the back:

"Get the old Welsh git! "

"Do 'im over! "

"Knock his head off! ! "

The crowd was by now dispersing rapidly, and Jones the Graves pulled Evans roughly from the bench.

"Come on! " he hissed, "let's get out of here! "

Flight into ? equals !!

"Quick, follow me! " shouted Victoria, and grasping Michael O'Donahue by the arm, she led the way through the throng, followed by Jones the Graves, pulling along a fuming Evans Motors, Jones the Smallholding, helping the pigtailed lady with her bundles and Stanley Hoxton, who still managed to continue his political argument with the long haired young lads as he ran.

Victoria ducked into a little alley that ran between two big stores, the one on the left closed down and boarded up. The others followed her, their hurried footfalls resounding and echoing against the walls at either side, and seeming louder in the narrow space between the buildings. They raced past a dry clearer's and a tobacconist's on one side, and a wool shop on the other, down the alleyway that was closed to all except pedestrians. At the far end they could see two painted signs hung out over the alley at first floor level, one from each side. The one on the left read 'The Moka Bar and Cafe', and the one on the right 'The Grapes Tavern'.

"Come on! Into the Grapes, quickly! " shouted Victoria, though there was as yet no sign of pursuit.

Directly below the two hanging signs, in the centre of the alleyway, and partly blocking it, there was a sturdy wooden barrier. This was intended to prevent anyone running, or blundering without looking, into the little street that here cut across the end of the alley at right angles, making a dangerous blind corner crossing necessary in order to reach the wider pedestrianised safety of Church Street that was the alleyway's continuation, going down towards the Cathedral.

Evans Motors crashed heavily into this barrier in his headlong haste to keep up with the others, and paused for a moment to read the words printed boldly on it.

"Beware of Vehicles! " he read aloud. Then he added: "You've got to beware of a lot of things in these big towns," and he disengaged himself from the obstacle muttering: "Beware of barriers, that's more to the point."

But without further mishap he followed his friends into the Grapes, which stood on the nearside corner of the little street.

"Well, we seem to have given them the slip," he puffed, as he entered.

"Yes," said Jones the Graves, only a little less out of breath. "I think we've thrown them off. But I wouldn't call it a pub crawl any more. It's become more of a pub trot! "

"We'll be all right in here," announced Victoria. "I've got friends in this pub."

The deafening thunder of a jukebox drowned all further conversation, as they passed through a wood-panelled lobby with an off-licence hatch, old-fashioned posters, and mirrors painted with Victorian advertisements on the walls. A prominently displayed sign read:

"Warning: be on the look out for suspicious parcels, or packages left in this pub. They may contain a bomb."

"What's that all about? " asked Michael O'Donahue.

"Oh, the Special Services boys come in here a lot. This is their local," replied Victoria.

The now further enlarged numbers of the party filed into the small bar to the right of the lobby, immediately making it crowded. The jukebox continued to blast out one hit after another, and Jones the Graves remarked:

"That thing's so loud I wouldn't hear a bomb if one went off right next to me."

"Don't you be so sure of that," said Stanley Hoxton.

The leaded, small-paned windows that took up most of the street wall, were made of a glass that could not be seen through, but which refracted the street lights outside into a pleasing diamond-like pattern on the inside, where a strong wire mesh had been fastened from top to bottom.

"Who's buying this round? " asked Jones the Graves.

"You should have read the sign over there before saying that! " Evans Motors laughed, pointing to a notice on the wall that read:

'BEFORE OPERATING MOUTH
ENSURE BRAIN IS ENGAGED'

"You said you'd buy the next round, remember? " the Motors continued.

"Oh come on," said Jones the Smallholding. "It's too big a round for one man now."

"Every man for himself, then, is it? " shouted Stanley Hoxton, but true to the spirit of the night, he bought the two long haired young men a drink. Their conflicting principles did not require them to refuse his offer. As he handed them their glasses, Mr. Hoxton asked them their names.

"Jake," said the one who had spoken back on the bench in High Town.

"Susie," said the other.

"Good Lord!" exclaimed Stanley Hoxton, staring at her. "You must excuse me. I thought you were a feller. Now I look closely, of course, I can see you're a girl. Well, that's a turn up for the book! It's usually me mistaking lads for lasses, with all this long hair they have today. I've never mistaken a lass for a lad before. I usually know a girl when I see one! I'm sorry, no offence meant of course. I mean, you're far too pretty to be a feller, now I see you close up and in the light. I thought you were a pretty boy, that's all."

"It doesn't bother me at all Mr. Hoxton," replied Susie. And Jake, with his arm round her shoulders, continued good naturedly if somewhat satirically:

"You see, Mister Stanley Hoxton, old fruit, we all need to get liberated from these hard and fast sexual role games. They're definitely yesterday's papers, which as you know, are full of bad news. I mean every man has something of a woman in him and every woman something of a man. If you deny this in yourself, you can become very unbalanced as a person and you'll never be able to truly know and respect the opposite sex."

Jones the Graves, who was standing at the bar listening, chipped in:

"Well, well, I never thought of that. You reckon I should get an apron and a pinafore then?"

Evans Motors pulled his friend's cap down over his eyes. "Oh, hark at him! Proper little comedian, aren't you, Jonesy? Didn't know you had it in you!"

"Don't be vulgar," Jones the Graves quipped back.

"Well, I was always taught that a man should be a man, and that being manly was a virtue," said Stanley Hoxton. Susie shook her head.

"I'm afraid you've missed the point, Mr. Hoxton," she said.

"You've become a plastic man!" jibed Jake.

Michael O'Donahue cut in before the conversation could descend to abuse.

"As far as I'm concerned," he said, "everyone should be just as they please, including Mr. Hoxton. However, I myself have learned to trust the natural instincts with which the good Lord has thankfully endowed me. And I have thus far found these instincts to be present in most young ladies, which is a truly fulfilling thing, and a never ending source of wonder to me!" He then returned his attention to his Guinness.

"I know what Jake and Susie are trying to say though," said Victoria. "I mean, it's hard to be you if other people treat you like something you're not. You can find yourself having to live with other people's preconceptions of you, and their expectations that come from this false image can really tie you up in knots. The whole idea of having to be 'ladylike' can be a real bore, when you just feel like anyone else."

"That's well said, my dear," the lady with the pigtail chipped in. "Just do as you please, be yourself, and let others get on with it." And then she introduced herself to the company.

"My name's Rose, by the way, though a lot of people calls me Rosie."

"Rose by any other name," laughed Jones the Smallholding, "would be as sweet."

Evans Motors put on a peculiarly mincing voice, and camped a few steps down the bar, rolling his backside to the booming bass of the jukebox.

"If anyone finds some silors tonight, please save one for me! " he said, to which Jones the Smallholding remarked:

"I didn't know this was a navy town. Stop prancing about, Evans, you'll do yourself a mischief, or get us thrown out of here.

But Evans continued to camp it up.

"Look here, my dears, you simply do not understand my finer feelings."

This was the cause of much mirth, to all except Stanley Hoxton, who seemed embarrassed.

"Get a grip on yourself, man! " he shouted.

"I'd sooner get a grip on you, dear," Evans retorted, and so saying, he took a firm grasp on Stanley Hoxton, murmuring breathily: "Darling, I think they're playing our tune. Shall we dance? " After which, amid general laughter he waltzed the indignant Stanley Hoxton round the bar. A chorus of ribald remarks erupted:

"Get 'em off, Evans, lass! "

"Show him your tango! ! "

"What about a rumba! ! "

When Evans finally let go, the beetroot faced Stanley Hoxton spluttered and fumed to himself. Evans, returning to his normal character and voice, slapped him on the back.

"Oh, come on Stanley, no hard feelings, eh? "

"Get away with you! " came the furious reply.

"Oh no! ! Don't go all broody on me! It was just a bit of fun! Remember the spirit of fun! "

"Oh, very well." Stanley forced a smile. Evans bought him another drink, to soothe his rumpled feathers, and they shook hands like firm friends.

Jake and Susie had retired over to the jukebox where, with Jake, or was it Susie, sat on the machine, they were locked in a lingering kiss, their long hair entwining, and hiding their faces, as they swayed to the music.

At a table in the corner, Victoria and Michael O'Donahue sat in a huddle, their noses not an inch away from each other, looking into each other's eyes, as they talked.

And Jones the Smallholding was enrapt in conversation with the lady with the pigtail, whose bundles occupied several chairs next to her.

"Seems to be quite a night for it, doesn't it," remarked Evans Motors with a grin. "What about you and me, Stanley? "

"Don't you start that again," replied the latter sternly, "or I shall begin to have serious doubts about you, Evans."

"Well perhaps love is the answer to all the questions we've been asking ourselves," said Jones the Graves, wistfully into his beer.

"I always said you should have been a parson! " laughed Evans.

"And you should have been the Pope! " retorted Jones the Graves rudely.

"Let's go through into the other bar, and leave this lot to it," said Stanley Hoxton.

This they did, and the stuffed stags' heads, stuffed birds, and brass bugles on display, were the cause of further jokes in dubious taste. They ordered another round, and took in the scene. A cluster of pretty, smartly dressed, young girls, hovered round the jukebox laughing amongst themselves, and moving in time to the music. They giggled uncontrolably at Evans' approach, and politely declined the Welsh veteran's invitation to dance.

"No luck, eh? " said a young Scotsman standing by the bar, as Evans returned to join his friends.

"Never mind, Evans, old boy," consoled Jones the Graves. "There's plenty of pubs left in this town. Why don't we carry on to the next one? The Last Great Pub Crawl cannot be allowed to grind to a standstill! "

"You on a pub crawl? " asked the Scotsman. And after the notion of the night was put to him plainly, he said: "I wouldn't mind joining you, if you've no objection. I'm just back from Northern Ireland, and I've seen some pretty terrible things over there."

"Well lad," said Stanley Hoxton. "It's blokes like you, who don't shrink from clearing up the messes other people make, that win my admiration every time. "

The soldier shook his head sadly, and replied:

"It's not a pretty business, I must say. You get to see the worst side of human nature come to the surface, and no mistake. Fear and hatred, pride and jealousy, and all that follows from them. I've seen more than my share of bloodshed, and bodies lying in the street. Bombs going off when you least expect them, children cut by flying glass, mothers screaming, sirens wailing, and innocent people injured, in a quarrel they want no part of. It's all snipers and snoopers these days. You just don't know who's a friend and who's an enemy at all.

I've been in all different parts of the world, while I've been in the Service, and believe me, that dark side of human nature doesn't change, whatever the colour of the skin, or the climate. I've seen just about every kind of dirty trick one human being can play on another, and I've had a bellyful of it. It'd do me good to go on a pub crawl, and get it out of my system! "

"Sounds like our little village isn't so bad after all," said Jones the Graves, turning to Evans, "it seems to have sheltered us from quite a few things. Perhaps that's what you gain to make up for the loss of being so cut off from the rest of the world."

"Oh yes, that's true enough," replied Evans, with a smile, "but don't forget Mrs. Owen and Mrs. Williams! There's sharpshooting tongues, if you like! "

"Well anyway," said Jones the Graves, turning back to the soldier, "you're welcome to join us. But we do have an Irishman, albeit one from the South, already aboard for the trip, and we trust there'll be no bad feeling."

"None on my part," said the soldier, and without further ado, they returned to the smaller bar, to mobilize the others. As they walked in, Jones the Graves shouted out:

"I propose a motion, that we set ourselves, and the Last Great Pub Crawl in motion! " He looked pleased as punch with his pun.

"Motion seconded! " shouted Evans Motors.

"Carried! " shouted Stanley Hoxton.

"Who needs to be carried? " asked Jones the Smallholding, already with his arms full of bundles. "No one's had that much to drink, yet, have they? "

Evans Excels

While it was certainly true that no one needed to be carried, as they issued forth from 'The Grapes', and crossed over the little road into Church Street, it was certainly also true that there was, nevertheless, definite evidence of a swagger here, and a stagger there. And the odd stumble, and the occasional hop, skip, or jump, betrayed the quantity already imbibed by the various members of the original party.

In any event, no sign was seen of the football fans, who were, no doubt, rampaging elsewhere in the night, and it was but a short step across the way into the Lichfield Vaults, whose door was open and welcoming. Victoria led them down a corridor, and through into the back bar.

Here, after the Scotsman was introduced to one and all as, quite logically, 'Scotty' Douglas, a darts match was proposed. Several wooden tables around the darboard were duly commandeered by Jake and Susie, who seemed to know most of the mainly blue jeaned young people in this bar. These regulars did not appear at all surprised by the strange company that had entered their local.

The jukebox played rather more quietly, much to the relief of Jones the Graves, who still complained that every song on it sounded much the same to him. He went over and examined the machine, but could neither unravel the names of most of the artists, nor decipher the titles. He was also at a loss as to how the machine worked.

"Bloody space age mumbo jumbo," he muttered to himself. "Fleetwood Mac? Pink Floyd? What on earth can they be? "

A small vole-like man, in an outsized overcoat, evidently on a very different circuit of the pubs of the City, approached and tried to interest him in buying a grubby pamphlet, relating to an obscure Christian sect, apparently emanating from Korea. Jones the Graves, despite his interest in general matters of the Church, politely declined to be drawn into a theological dialogue. He disengaged himself from the jukebox, and the man in the overcoat, and rejoined his friends, who were stood in a line, with elbows on the bar, and boots on the brass rail beneath it.

"What are we drinking, then? " he enquired.

"Let's try something out of the ordinary! " shouted Stanley Hoxton. "If you can think of something suitably exotic, I'll buy it! "

"What about rum? " someone shouted.

"Too ordinary," was Stanley Hoxton's prompt verdict.

"Brandy? "

"Too ordinary! "

"Grenadine? "

"Too sickly! "

"Cinzano? "

"No."

"Vodka? "

"No."

"What about a couple of bottles of Tequila! " shouted Jake.

"What's that? " asked Jones the Smallholding. "I thought it was a dance! "

"It's a Mexican drink, very tasty," replied Jake.

"Sounds a great idea," said Michael O'Donahue, who had been talking to the Scottish soldier, and appeared to be getting on very well with him.

"I've never tried Tequila," said Evans Motors.

"Try anything once, love, and live to tell the tale! " shouted Rosie, from where she sat, next to Victoria, on the leather bench that ran along the end wall, with her bundles in a row beside her.

"Tequila it is! " decided the generous Hoxton.

The bottles were bought, and opened, and the glasses were filled. Jake made a great point of showing everyone how to take each drink with a pinch of salt, supplied by the barman, but Evans decided the idea would not catch on in the land of his fathers. Then the darts teams were drawn up, and the game began.

"Your singing was great back there in the main square," said Michael O'Donahue to Rosie, between shots at the double top.

"Oh, I'm no great shakes love," she replied, "but you're a right fine whistle player, an' that's for certain. You've not been long in town have you? "

"No, I just got a ride down from Holyhead yesterday," said Michael.

"Will you be stopping long? " Rosie winked, and nudged Victoria, who blushed. Michael smiled and said:

"Well now, we'll have to see about that. I've not stopped in one place long, for quite a while now. But you never know, something might come along and make me change me ways. What about you, Rosie, me dear, where are you from? "

"Oh, nowhere in particular, at the moment, love. I've been doin' the hop pickin'. I've got a little trailer, an' I do the rounds. It's interesting to see different places. I make enough in the summers to see me tidy through the winters. I've got a little patch where I can pull off the road till the spring comes round again."

"This Tequila's pretty strong stuff, isn't it? " said Victoria, as one of her darts missed the board completely, and stuck firmly into the wall.

"That's right, blame it on the booze," said Stanley Hoxton, teasingly.

"Let's see you do better then, champ," said Jake, "and don't think I've finished with you yet. By the time you go on your way after tonight, you'll know more about Chairman Mao, than Enoch Powell knows about intolerance."

"Cheeky devil," chuckled Stanley.

Evans Motors scored the first bullseye, and couldn't get over it. He swashbuckled around the bar, inviting every young lady in it to dance, but was declined on all sides. This was hardly surprising, as he was now suffering from an extraordinary attack of the hiccups, which made his mountainous bulk quiver volcanicly.

"Careful Evans, don't go hiccuping all over those girls, you'll frighten them to death," remarked Jones the Graves. "I think you must be losing your touch with the ladies, you know."

"Nonsense! " shouted Victoria. "He's too good for them all! "

"Hic, thank you my dear," said Evans. "Spoken, hic, like a true, hic, friend! "

By the time the darts game came to an end, after a close fought finish, with Evans Motors' team coming out on top, the bottles of Tequila were dry, and they were, indeed, all becoming true friends. The nature of intoxication being such as it is, they might very well have befriended anyone, and everyone, in the entire world.

Evans, having somehow got rid of his hiccups, lurched into the centre of the room, from where he launched into an epic limerick, of the sort that he had been famous for at school. This one was, however, rather more bawdy, and, raising his glass, he delivered it so loudly that he outpowered the jukebox.

"Here's a toast to all
the girls of the valley,
to all the girls of the village,
and all the girls of the city!

To all ladies and women,
married and single,
kissed and unkissed,
lovers and leftovers,
to the virtuous chaste,
and to the not so virtuous
that get married in haste!

Here's to the gentle caress
of a hand on a breast,
to the pat of a bum,
the pinch of a cheek,
and to the twinkle
in the wink of an eye
that says all you need,
without you having to speak.

Here's to the slap and tickle,
the squirm and the wriggle,
the tease and the flirt,
the common as dirt,
the snooty and haughty,
the nice and the naughty.

Here's to the schoolgirl crush,
the maidenly blush,
the look in the mirror
when nobody's there,
and the magic feeling
of a first affair.

Here's to the backseat of the car,
the back row of the dark cinema,
and the ooh la la!
Here's to the stocking, the shocking,
the girdle and garter,
the 'ooh, you didn't oughter!',
and to the 'love me some more', after.

Here's to 'my place or yours?
behind closed curtains and doors;
here's to the big double bed,
to the sofa,
and, of course, the divan;
and here's to all the reasons
the seduction didn't go
quite according to plan.

Here's to the roly poly,
not so holy,
rub-a-dub-dub,
there's two in the tub.

Here's to the naked,
caught napping,
nearly got away with it,
lovers who lay in the loft,
moaning like cats in a copse;
and here's to the roll in the hay,
the night in the barn
that never did anyone
any harm.

Here's to the nude,
to the rude,
to the nibble,
the navel,
the nipple,
and the whole human body,
in its wonder and marvel.

Here's to the negligee
the nighty,
the knicker elastic,
the bra, and the panty;
Here's to rum joke,
and the belly laughs,
and to the man in the brown mac,
with the dirty photographs.

Here's to the mothers
with babies in bellies,
here's to the glamour girl models
we see on our tellies,
and here's to the farm girls
in their dungarees
and their wellies.

In short, here's to all lovers,
from back street mistresses,
to misters and missus,
from the very first kiss,
to forty years wedded bliss!"

Having got that off his chest, Evans Motors was well warmed up, and the room was in uproar. But he was not finished yet.

"I am now possessed of a great desire to sing! " he announced.

"As long as that's the only desire you're possessed by, we should be all right," said Stanley Hoxton.

Undaunted, Evans launched into the chorus of 'Men of Harlech', and as a point of honour the two Joneses, felt obliged to join in. And very fine it was, too, until they were politely asked to leave by the barman, whose patience had been tried too far.

"But we were just getting going! " pleaded Evans.

"Well do me a favour and get gone! " the barman replied, firmly.

"Where can we go and play some more music? " asked Michael O'Donahue.

"I know just the place," said Victoria. "There's another folk club down in the Black Lion in Bridge Street. Let's go there. It's a bit of a walk, but it'll be worth it."

Victoria Tours (Continued)

This time as they left the pub, there was a distinct nautical roll in the way they walked, as if they were at sea in a heavy swell. A straight line may well be the shortest direction between two points, but it was getting harder for them to be able to say exactly what a straight line was. Even Scotty, the soldier, who had been the last to join them, was beginning to lose touch with what is normally known as reality.

"Lead the way, Victoria," commanded Stanley Hoxton.

"Male chauvinist pig! " shouted Jake and Susie together.

"New kind of imported bacon, is it? " asked Jones the Graves.

"Never heard of that breed of porker," said Jones the Smallholding, still bearing bundles, "and I've kept a few pigs in me time! "

"Where have you guys been for the last ten years? " asked Jake. "Have you been living in another world? "

"You might be right there," answered Evans Motors, as he zigzaged down Church Street, with Victoria on one arm and Rosie on the other, "but now we're making up for lost time."

Victoria disengaged herself from Evans, and began her guided tour again.

"As we resume our walk through this historic City, ladies and gentlemen, you will observe, on the left, the historic hi-fi shop, and historic cafe. On the right you will observe the excellent Society of Craftsmen's Craft Shop, the historic barber's, and the ever-expanding historic Hereford Bookshop. Note the historic plaque on the historic wall, concerning the fact that a historic mayor, historically, lived here."

The others followed, falling about and laughing, as she lead the way.

"On the left again, we pass by the high walls of the garden of The South Hereford Unionist Association. Note the brass nameplate. And on the right hand side here, you will observe the historic Telephone Exchange.

Taking care not to impale yourselves on the historic railings that you see here acting as a barrier across the end of Church Street, you will note, as you pass through the gate, the immortal words of the bard, inscribed for posterity on this board:

'Cycling in the Close is not permitted.'

How succinctly those words express their author's sentiment. In the hands of such a master, so little can say so much! "

Victoria's monologue had them all in stitches, as the ten of them filed one by one through the gate in the railings, out of the narrow cobbled confines of Church Street, and into the wide open expanse of the Cathedral Close.

Beyond the neat lawns and tarmaced paths, the dark mass of the Cathedral loomed before them, rising grand and stately out of the pools of light thrown by the Victorian street lamps among the spreading trees. It was an inspiring sight, needing no comment, and Victoria fell silent.

Held still in stone, the master mason's ingenuity arched its back, vaulted through space, and towered above them, pushing pinnacles towards the night sky.

A single light shone above an iron-studded door, set in an arched entranceway, and the reflections of the street lights danced on the outside of the unlit stained glass windows. These were the only punctuations to the black shape of the great old building, before which the company stood in silence for a while, each one lost in his own thoughts.

Then Jones the Graves spoke:

"Lot of work to keep all this grass tidy," he said, and everyone laughed.

"Trust you to think of that," said Jones the Smallholding, "but I suppose I'm no better. I was thinking of my work, too, and about my land. It still seems marvellous to me how a great tree can grow from a tiny seed, and how the seasons each come in their turn, bringing their changes to the earth. I was thinking about all the tiny creatures that live in the soil, and wondering if they felt useful, and I was thinking of my goats, and cows and chickens, and wondering if they miss me, and what they'll do when I retire. I can't help but ask myself what it will be like to see my old place lived in by someone else. It makes me sad to think they'll probably tart the house up, and tidy it all up, and I shan't recognise it when I visit. But I'm glad we came on this journey, you know, it had to be done. You look at things quite differently when you get away for a while."

Rosie put her hand on his arm when he stopped speaking, and he smiled at her.

"Yes," said Evans Motors, "there was a great necessity for this adventure. I was just wondering why my old bus wouldn't start this afternoon! It's funny how you carry all this stuff around in your head, and somehow all of it is what you think of as you. Your past, the things you own, the friends you've known, they're all in your head, I suppose, so they're with you wherever you go. It's very strange. You know, I think I've been so busy being Evans Motors that I've never had much time to think about who he really is. Does he really exist at all, I wonder, separate from that damn garage? Will he vanish into thin air the day he retires? ! "

"I very much doubt it," said Stanley Hoxton, drily. "If he vanishes at all, it'll be into hot air. Your ale-fired reminiscences are very fascinating, I'm sure, but I'm beginning to get hungry. And that sort of speculation doesn't go down too well on an empty stomach, awash with booze. Is there anywhere we can get something to eat, Victoria? "

Victoria gave this question some thought in befuddled silence, and Michael O'Donahue said:

"What about this folk club you were talking about? I'd just like to get down there."

Then standing in front of the Cathedral, he began to play a jig on his whistle, to which Jake and Susie danced, between the rose beds, in a flailing frenzy of flying arms and legs.

"Time's marching on," said Jones the Graves, looking at his watch as if he'd never seen it before, despite the fact that he had wound it every night at exactly ten p.m. for the last forty odd years, setting it to the chimes of Big Ben on the radio.

"I'll tell you what," said Victoria, "We can get something from the Chinese takeaway place, and eat it on the way down to the folk club. That'll keep everybody happy, I should imagine."

Just then they heard shouting in the distance, and could quite clearly make out the chanting of the football supporters. Evans walked over towards the City Museum and Library, on the other side of the road, and looked down Broad Street. Then he turned, and came running back.

"It's the same lot as before! " he shouted. "They must still be after me. I think they saw me! "

"Come on then! " yelled Victoria. "This way, quickly! "

And they all ran together, past the Palace Yard Bookshop, into the dark and narrow embrace of Gwynne Street. A high stone wall flanked one side of the little road, and a terraced row of small red brick artisans cottages, each with a hedged and gated garden, flanked the other.

"Watch out for cars coming the other way! " yelled Jake. "They're on top of you before you know it, coming round that corner! "

"Are they still following us? " puffed Evans, as he ran, not feeling steady enough on his feet to risk looking over his shoulder himself, whilst in motion.

"Who are we running away from anyway? " asked a bewildered Scotty, obviously in a fitter condition than all the others put together.

"Hooligans! " shouted Stanley Hoxton.

"Soccer thugs! " said Jones the Smallholding. "I always was a rugby man, meself! "

Which was just as well, as he was now obliged to run carrying an armful of bundles.

They clattered on past another plaque, set in the stone wall to the left, which read:

'City of Hereford. Site of the birth place of Nell Gwynne. Mother of
the first Duke of St. Albans. Founder of the Chelsea hospital. Born
1650, died 1691.'

"That's a polite way of putting it," wheezed Stanley Hoxton. "We all know about her, and her oranges! "

"Save your breath," shouted Jake.

But then Jones the Smallholding, lagging behind a little with Rosie, called out:

"I don't think they're coming this way at all, you know! ", and slowed to a walk.

"You can't be too careful," replied Evans Motors, thinking of the empty can bouncing off his head. But he too stopped running, after several cautious glances behind him.

"Well, that's twice we've shown them a clean pair of heels," sake Jake. "I reckon the next time they show up, we should see 'em off."

"Big words, lad," said Stanley Hoxton, 'but in my humble opinion your generation's too soft to fight a butterfly. If you had to fight a war like us lot did, heaven help the free world, that's all I say."

"Do me a favour, and stop talking about fighting," Scotty complained. "I'd like to get away from it for a while, if you don't mind, seeing as I'm on leave."

Before anyone could say anything further, they had followed the curve of Gwynn Street to the point where it met the wider thoroughfare of Bridge Street at right angles. Directly in front of them, on the opposite side of the road, was the half-timbered, gabled front of the Black Lion.

"Is that where the folk club is? " asked Michael O'Donahue.

"It is," answered Victoria. "Do you think we should go straight in there, and get off the street? "

"No, no," said Stanley Hoxton. "I'm far too hungry for that. Besides we're not going to let a bunch of hooligans prevent us enjoying ourselves, are we? I think they've put our noses out enough for one night already. Anyway, there's no sign of them now. I think we've lost them again. So where's this Chinese place, or whatever you were talking about? "

"It's just up there on the left," said Victoria, pointing up the street.

They sauntered slowly up past an off-licence, till they came to the Crystal Rooms. This cabaret nightspot appealed to Stanley Hoxton.

"Looks a good place," he said. "How about going in here? I'll bet you can get a decent meal, and some proper entertainment."

"I've never been in there," answered Victoria. And as the dress of several of them, and the amount of alcohol consumed by all of them, left a great deal to be desired for this particular establishment, they passed it by, crossed over the road by the launderette, and approached the Chinese takeaway restaurant.

A red and green neon sign shone from the window, reading 'Chop Suey Bar', and an appetising smell wafted out onto the pavement.

Chop Suey Chaos

Jones the Graves stared in through the window of the Chop Suey Bar at the Chinaman behind the counter, who was reading the evening paper. A fruit machine stood beneath a large menu stuck up on the wall.

"Do they speak English in there? " the Graves wondered aloud.

"Probably better than you do," said Stanley Hoxton. Evans Motors laughed.

"Do you suppose this could be my first experience of the ancient wisdoms of the mysterious East? " he said.

"What sort of food do they serve? " asked Jones the Smallholding, with a distinct note of uncertainty in his voice.

"Oh, curries, chop suey, these places have most things usually," answered Stanley Hoxton, feeling quite the man of the world

He put his foot on the bottom of the two steps, tripped over the next one, and went flying in through the door, ending up in a crumpled heap in front of the raised counter at the far side of the room.

The Chinese man who sat behind the counter smiled down at him over the top of his glasses.

"Can I help you, sir? What would you like, sir? " he asked politely.

The others had by now entered, and they helped Mr. Hoxton to his feet, trying hard not to hurt his feelings by doubling up with laughter at his undignified, though acrobatic, entrance. Stanley Hoxton himself seemed a little dazed, but otherwise undamaged.

The ensuing process of sorting out the order for ten considerably inebriated people, and putting that order into a form that could be understood by the Chinaman, proved to be a very exacting one.

"Two beef curries."

"Er, one chop suey."

"One vegetable curry here."

"Yes sir, that's two chop sueys, one vegetable curry, one beef curry, two chicken curries ..."

"No wait a minute, make that three chicken curries, and anyway wasn't it two beef curries? "

"Yes sir, that's three chicken curries, one chop suey ..."

"Hey, who else wants chips! I want chips with my chop suey ..."

"Yes, I'll have chips."

"So will I."

"None for me."

Somehow the Chinese gentleman managed to remain polite and patient throughout. But peering coyly out from the kitchen hidden behind a curtain to the rear, two Chinese ladies could be seen nearly collapsing with laughter at the chaos that reigned below.

"How many chop sueys? "

"We'll need some plastic spoons."

"Have you got any tomato ketchup? "

"Don't get in my way, Evans, I'm trying to see the menu! "

Eventually it was all written down on the little pad, the order was passed up to the kitchen, and the bill was settled with much further confusion over the change. Then,when the foil containers of food were finally passed down, it naturally took some time to sort out exactly what was in which, and for each hot package to reach the person who had requested it.

"I didn't order jellied eels," complained Evans Motors.

"That's bean shoots! They're mine," laughed Victoria. "Give them over here! "

"Funny sort of grub," said Jones the Graves, as they stumbled out into the street, and walked slowly back down towards the Blank Lion, spoons in hand, gobbling and guzzling like gluttons. They laid into the food with such gusto that by the time they reached the pub, this being the sixth of the night, the last drops of sauce were being slurped noisily down, and the odd belch could be heard to rudely rend the air, hastily followed by overdone, and not very sincere, apologies.

"Urp! I do most humbly beg your gracious pardon," rumbled Michael O'Donahue.

"Granted," replied Evans Motors.

"This way! " shouted Victoria. "The folk club's round the back and upstairs."

They dumped their food containers in a litterbin, and followed her into the cobblestoned yard beside the pub. A few cars were parked tight up against the walls, and music drifted from a doorway.

"Hey, fellers, there's a gents here, if anyone needs it before we go up! "

announced Jake.

"Good idea! "

"Just what the doctor ordered! "

"Wonderful! "

"Excellent suggestion! ", came the replies, and those that could squeeze in jostled their way into the little gents off the courtyard, where the sound of hissing pipes and gurgling cysterns awaited them. The others formed a queue outside.

"Tell me," said Jones the Graves to Evans Motors, as they stood within, obtaining much needed relief with great sighs, "how will we know when we've reached the end of this pub crawl? "

"Oh," replied Evans. "We'll see a sign."

"A sign? " queried the Graves.

"Yes," said Evans Motors with conviction. "Some sort of sign! "

Jones the Smallholding, standing next to them at the fixture, was peering at something on the wall in front of him. 'Look up! ' it said. He did so, and written just above head level was the following comment:

'If you can read this you're probably peeing in your turnups.'

Uproar as Before

When one and all had duly answered the calls of nature, they made their way in through the door, and began to climb the steep flight of steps to the club above. This was a task that could prove difficult at the best of times, but in their present conditon, it involved a more than usual effort.

"Don't push! " shouted Stanley Hoxton, colliding with Evans.

"Michael, pull me up! " giggled Victoria, as she slipped and nearly lost her footing. He took the opportunity to grasp her firmly round the waist, and kiss her passionately. They swayed dangerously, lost to the world. Coming up behind, Rosie bumped into them and lost her grip on her bundles, which bounced down the stairs, crashing into Jones the Graves, sending him flying. Jones the Smallholding tripped while trying to turn back to help his namesake, and the bundles he was carrying rained down on the unfortunate sexton.

"Help! " shouted the Graves. "I'm being murdered! "

"Help! " laughed Jones the Smallholding. "Send the Saint Bernards! Mountain rescue required! "

"Ssh! " hissed someone from the top of the stairs. "Not so much noise. There is music going on inside, you know."

The mysterious bundles had burst open, scattering a large quantity of old fashioned ladies underwear, stockings, socks, woollen vests, handkerchieves, tea towels, and assorted linen all over the place. Jones the Graves sat up, uninjured, but with a large pair of drawers over his head.

"What in Heaven's name? " he asked.

"Me clean washing, me clean washing! " lamented Rosie, but it did not take long for Scotty, Jake and Susie to help her gather it all together again.

Somehow or other they finally reached the top of the stairs, where they were admitted to the club without paying.

"It's getting late, anyway," said the blond young man on the door. But the chaos he envisaged in attempting to take money from this extraordinary collection of people may well have been the deciding factor.

"Just go on inside," he said, as if he thought it lucky that the whole place had not been turned upside down.

And so all ten of them went through the door into the little square room with a bar that adjoined the old skittle alley in which the music was now being played. Posters for various folk singers and groups adorned one wall, but they paid no attention to these, being more interested in getting something to drink after the spicy food they had just consumed.

"Great, they've got the draught stuff up here! " exulted Michael O'Donahue, and with his drink in one hand, and Victoria's hand in the other, he pushed his way up the two steps, through the open sliding door, and into the back of the crowded club.

"'Scuse me, 'scuse me," he muttered, as they elbowed through the crowd, towards a large battered old sofa at one side, that still remained unoccupied. They sat down and took in the scene.

It was a long, low, dimly-lit room, with the exposed beams of the roof trusses making big triangles in the ceiling, which had a raised glass skylight in its centre. Benches, tables, and chairs were scattered about at the sides, filled with the shadowy shapes and figures of the night's audience. A gangway ran down the middle, and at the far end, a single spotlight pierced the smoky haze, shining on the performing area, behind which a curtain was hung. A clean-shaven young man, with a twinkle in his eye, and a large curious shaped cap on his head, was standing in his wellington boots at centre stage. He was playing a well travelled guitar, and singing a song whose chorus was well enough known to the whole club for them to join in with it. Even the new arrivals soon picked up the words, which were particularly apt, running something like this:

"Its all for me beer,
me jolly, jolly beer,
it's all for me beer
and tobaccer;
I've spent all me tin
on the lassies drinkin' gin,
and across the Western Ocean
I must wander."

Evans Motors was standing at the back singing along, beer in hand, and friends around. When the song ended, he shouted out in Welsh thunder:

"Let's hear Michael O'Donahue! "

"Who's Michael O'Donahue? " asked the man in the spotlight, as the applause subsided, and all heads turned to look at Evans, who yelled back:

"Michael O'Donahue is a fine whistle player from Dublin! "

"Well, let's hear him then," shouted the wellington booted singer.

Michael stumbled to the fore, found his way somehow into the spotlight beam, grinned sheepishly at those around him, put the whistle to his lips, and for the second time, this Saturday night, his music silenced a crowded room. He stood with his eyes shut tight, bobbing up and down to the beat, and gradually, as he wove his spell, the rhythm hypnotised every person in the place.

The regulars of the club were at first surprised by the spectacle of three elderly Welshmen dancing arm in arm down the centre gangway, followed in a line by a silver-haired Yorkshire businessman, a large lady with a pigtail, a pretty young blonde girl, two longhaired youngsters, and a Scottish soldier. Furthermore, a strong smell of curry seemed suddenly to have invaded the room. But it was not long before everyone was on their feet, laughing and dancing, as the carnival spirit took over.

When Michael finally stopped playing, leaving one long drawn-out soaring note hanging in the air, a great roar of approval, and shouts for more, filled the room. But he dodged away into the darkness towards the back, and Evans Motors took his place in the spotlight.

"My Lords, Ladies, and Gentlemen! " he bellowed, holding up his glass towards the ceiling. "I raise my glass to the great and glorious variety of alcoholic beverages known to man, to the wondrous and infinite variety of public houses in this country, and more particularly in this town. I propose a toast to the differences between us, and the great similarities! To the beasts of the fields, to the birds of the air, to the fish of the rivers and of the sea, and to all the creatures of creation! "

Jones the Smallholding butted in, bellowing too:

"Here's to the splendours of the Mountains of Wales! "

"To the moors of Yorkshire!" boomed Stanely Hoxton.

"To the Emerald Isle! " shouted Michael O'Donahue.

"To the highland heather! " added Scotty.

"To the City of Hereford! " came Victoria's clear voice.

"To the countryside all around it! " chirped Rosie.

"To freedom! " yelled Jake.

"To the liberation of women! " shouted Susie.

"No politics! " yelled Evans Motors.

"To the day that elephants fly! " shouted Jones the Graves. "Here's mud in your eye! "

"To the sun, to the moon! To the stars, and the wind and the rain! To the eye of the hurricane! To laughter and tears, and hopes and fears! To the past and the present, to the future and to history, to the whole universe in all its mystery! " summed up Jones the Smallholding.

"Last Orders! " shouted the landlord.

"To the Last Great Pub Crawl! " roared Evans Motors, in defiance.

"To the next pub! " concluded Victoria. "We'll have to be quick! "

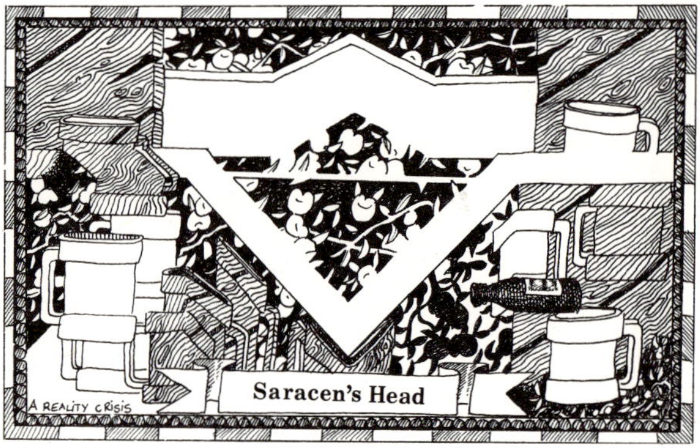

Visions and Voices

Swept off course, and carried along on the now flooding tide of The Last Great Pub Crawl, half the folk club followed as Victoria lead the way back down the stairs and out into the courtyard again, where the night air had grown crisp, and the stars shone brightly.

"Over the bridge," she yelled, arm in arm with Michael, who began to play his whistle once more. The motley crew made its way round the corner, and out into the street, hurrying towards the Saracen's Head.

"Follow the piper," called Jake to the Welshmen, who were lagging a little behind as the crowd of about twenty-five people, of all shapes and sizes, streamed onto the narrow, stone parapeted old bridge. A cool breeze came up from the river Wye below. The hum of traffic drifted over from the concrete span of the new bridge that carried the main road, running exactly parallel to the bridge they were crossing, a few hundred yards away, and slightly higher.

Jones the Graves stopped in one of the v-shaped recesses at the edge of the pavement, above the stone buttresses that carried the old bridge. He leaned on the wall, and looked down river at the lights of the houses reflected in the water, at the shadows of the gently waving willows, at the black sky, and at the Cathedral silhouetted against the stars.

"I feel marvellous," he said quietly to Evans and Jones the Smallholding, who had stopped beside him, "but I think I'm going to be sick."

"Don't worry, the fresh air will soon clear your head," whispered Evans, taking a firm grip on the back of the jacket of his lifelong friend.

"My head's spinning, my head's spinning," moaned Jones the Graves, "it won't stay still, it won't stay still!" And then he began to ramble. "I can hear voices ... voices ... voices ... calling me ... talking to me ...

I who have for so long now dug the graves and buried the dead of our one small village, I who have tended the flowers, and minded the stones placed above the departed ones, now seem to hear their voices calling out from the dark in the chapel of my brain. Each one unforgotten, though long gone, the old and the young, the wise and the wicked alike, a whole congregation of the dead, seems to be calling to me, shouting out: 'Jones awake! Jones awake! How long will you slumber? ' And they are laughing and singing in my skull, so that my thoughts will not be still. And now there's only one voice. It's my brother's, and he's saying: 'Listen, Dai Jones, you faithful watcher of dry bones, have you not dug the earth enough to know that no thing is, that does not have some life in it? Even the ground you walk on is living! Why, therefore, fear you to die? '

And now I hear another voice, a woman's voice, it's my own sweet Gracie, and she is saying: 'Jonesy, Jonesy, listen to me! How patient is the silence and this resting! How full is this emptiness, and how light this darkness now! Do not fear to lay down the burden you have for so long been carrying. All is well, all is well, and you are not forgotten.'

Now I can see them! They are all pointing their fingers at the sky! And someone is saying: 'Look at the stars, old Jones, you cannot see them in the daytime, yet still they are shining.'

And another voice is saying: 'Think of the sun, and wonder at the sound of its burning; think of the earth spinning round the sun, and try to hear the sound of its turning! '

And someone else is calling: 'Can you imagine the sound of the moon, as it spins, forever turning its shining face? Why have you come to feel yourself so alone surrounded by such signs of wonder and grace! '

Now all their voices are joined together, and they are singing!

'Each blade of grass,
each leaf of the tree,
each mouse, each bird, each worm,
all life flows ceaselessly back and forth
all forever in motion,
and each living thing, no matter how great or small,
is an inseparable part of the whole,
a drop in the boundless ocean. '

And now they are silent ... I can't see them any more ... they've gone . they've gone! Where am I? "

"You're here on the bridge, with me and Evans," said Jones the Smallholding, putting his arm round the Graves' shoulders, "and everything's just fine."

"I suppose you'll tell me I'm a drunken old fool," said the Graves, but the other two just looked at him, smiling and saying nothing. Then Evans Motors laughed, and shouted:

"Jones the Graves, boy, I always said you should have been a parson! You know I haven't felt like this since I was a boy romping and stomping round that old village in the hills, or running on the seaside sands in the summers, splashing in the sea. There's a great weight been lifted from me tonight! We've been too long in harness, you know, and it's time we went out to clover. Let the youngsters take over! "

"That's true, Evans," said Jones the Smallholding quietly. "I've started to quite look forward to heing able to roam about wherever I like, without all those animals to tie me down to one place. I don't think I'll be going to me sister's after all. I've been talking to Rosie, and we've a lot in common, you know. She's got her caravan, and I've got me savings put by, and what with one thing and another..."

But then a shout from Victoria interrupted him.

"Are you lot coming? " she yelled from outside the pub at the other side of the bridge. "Michael's already bought you some drinks, but if you don't hurry up it'll be closing time before you get to them! "

"We're on our way! " Evans shouted back.

"I'll be all right now," said Jones the Graves. "I thought my head was going to burst for a moment, back there, but I feel fine now. In fact, I've never felt better! "

And with a friend on each arm, he walked steadily across the bridge. When they got to the pub, the others made to go straight inside, but something had caught Jones the Graves' eye, and he stopped them.

"You were right, Evans," he smiled. "Look up there! "

They followed his gaze to a sign fixed on the wall. Not the fine pub sign that portrayed a turbaned Saracen's Head, but beyond that to a circular traffic sign.

The three old boys stood laughing on the pavement for a moment, before they went inside to sit, quietly now, to drink a last drink, think back on the night, and look forward to the future.

Inscribed on the traffic sign, beneath a red circle enclosing a diagram of two vehicles, one beside the other, was the single word:

'End.'

End